Hope at the Crossroads

Crissi Langwell

Hope Series

Book 2

Copyright © 2017 Crissi Langwell and
North Coast Stories

Image credit
Front image: Alex Prochkailo
Back image: Tomas Marek (Samot)
Inside bird image: 2kawaiiiness

ISBN-10: 0-9967717-4-3
ISBN-13: 978-0996771740

This book is also available as an e-book. Please visit the author's website to find out where you can purchase it.

crissilangwell.com

If it were not for hope, the heart would break.

~ Thomas Fuller

Table of Contents

1. A Normal Life 1

2. The Gardener 19

3. The Playdate 39

4. My Dirty Past 53

5. Falling in Like 71

6. Knocked-up Teen 83

7. Future Tripping 101

8. A Face From the Past 125

9. Permanent 141

10. Daddy's Girl 157

11. Bird 175

12. Good Together 187

13. Saying Goodbye 203

14. It's Complicated 221

15. Just a Game 227

16. Come With Me 243

Acknowledgements 249

Crissi's Books 251

A Normal Life

Summer vacation did not mean sleeping in—not for me, at least. On the first Monday after high school graduation, Charlie woke me up before the sun so I could learn how to prune the vines in the vineyard behind the house.

I got up quietly, the small lamp on my bedside table providing the only light in the room. Despite the chilly morning, I knew the June sun would be unrelenting later in the day, so I dressed in layers. Then I walked lightly past Hope's room, hoping my toddler would stay asleep for at least a few more hours.

In the kitchen, Fátima handed me a piece of toast smothered with smashed avocado, and then gave me a kiss on the cheek. She'd twisted her long, black hair into a thick bun on the top of her head, but a few tendrils had escaped and tickled my skin when she came close.

"Gracias," I whispered, and she nodded with a small smile before moving back to cutting board and several neat piles of vegetables. I watched her for a moment, amazed at the way she quickly chopped each vegetable into even slices. I loved this woman as an aunt, definitely as part of my extended family. In a few hours, the household would be bustling under her care. She'd help get Hope up and dressed, and would tend to Charlie's wife, Viola, while the rest of us worked outside. She was the reason I'd graduated high school; she'd cared for Hope while I went to class. And now, she made sure I could continue my studies, even if it was in a dark vineyard at an ungodly hour. She did so much for me, just as she did for everyone around her.

I heard the sliding door that led to the back open, and I turned as Charlie walked in, a cup of coffee at his lips. Despite how early it was, he looked as if he'd been away for hours. He wore his heavy jacket, the one with the thick, mustard-colored fabric that usually hung on the hook in his office during the heat of the day. His newsboy cap covered his thinning hair, and his blue eyes crinkled in the corners as he gave me an amused look. He knew I hated mornings.

"Hey Maddie," he said. "Are you ready?"

"Ready," I said. I chewed on the piece of toast as Charlie and I stepped outside. It took a moment for my eyes to adjust, but soon the whispering rows of darkened vines came into view, covering the hillside behind the Winston's house. As the sky went from purple to orange from the still-hidden sun, the green of the vines began to emerge.

I turned at the crunching of tires on the gravel roadway, and squinted in the light of the lead vineyard worker's truck. A few silhouettes crossed in front of the lights, and Charlie left me so he could talk with the crew.

"Come here so Manuel can show you how to pull the leaves," he called. I shyly made my way over, and then watched in the dim morning light as Manuel demonstrated what I'd be doing that morning. I studied his hands flying over the branches, pulling leaves at the bottom while leaving the grapes intact. Sometimes he'd tug at the wire, and Charlie explained he was correcting the cane so that it grew upward. Occasionally, Manuel pulled full branches out with the leaves, and I came to understand it was because they held no fruit. It was remarkable how fast he worked, knowing instinctively when to pull leaves or straighten branches. When it was my turn, I felt self-conscious at how slowly I moved in contrast to the workers around me. Charlie told me not to worry, but I still felt silly.

"This isn't about how fast you go," he told me, stopping my work so that I faced him. "This is so you understand what goes into making wine. Someday, when you're a vintner, this won't be a normal part of your job. But you should never forget the hard work it takes before the wine is poured out of the bottle."

I had three more months until my viticulture studies started, but Charlie hoped I'd be ahead of everyone in my classes. His ultimate goal was that I'd quickly learn the business so I could take over the winery one day. He was excited for me to be a part of his family business. However, I wasn't as eager as Charlie was. It wasn't that I wanted to lie around—that was impossible with a toddler. I just longed to get a job away from the house, meet new people, and learn new things. But to say anything to Charlie felt ungrateful. The Winstons had taken me in when no one else wanted me. They made sure Hope and I had everything we needed, and more. They even paid the part of my college tuition that grants and scholarships didn't cover. I owed them so much. Plus, Charlie's offer was a great opportunity. To want anything different seemed stupid and selfish. It was better to say nothing.

By midmorning, the sun was already beating down on those of us in the vines. My back ached from hours of pulling leaves and my hair stuck to the sweat on my neck, but I was happy with what I'd done. I looked down the line and noted how tidy it appeared.

"You've done good work." Charlie clapped his hand on my shoulder. I smiled and wiped my sweaty forehead. Despite my earlier feelings, I felt accomplished. It wasn't much, but the progress felt rewarding.

"How much more do I need to do?" I asked.

"Let the workers do it," he said. "Like I said, it's not so much what you get done but what you *learn*. If you're going to be a part of this business, it's important you know what it takes to run a vineyard."

I nodded. It made sense. Still, I wished I were as enthusiastic about this as he was. Maybe I'd change my mind once I started school.

"Come on," Charlie said, handing me a cool water from the ice chest at the end of the line. "Let's go cool off in my office and study vocabulary. Viticulture has its own language, and the sooner you learn it, the better."

I groaned inwardly as I took a long drink of the water. It left a cool trail through my body, making up for the heat around me. I finished it in three gulps, then tossed it in a bucket as I followed him back to the house.

The air inside was naturally cool, the adobe exterior keeping the house cool from the summer sun without need for air conditioning. I slipped off my shoes and socks once inside so I could feel the cold kitchen tile on my feet. I could hear Fátima talking with Hope in the laundry room, and I longed to be done working so I could take my daughter off Fátima's hands, but we headed straight toward Charlie's office instead. He closed the door and pulled out paperwork. He shuffled through the pages for a moment, and I waited to see what his next job was for me. He cleared his throat, and then pulled a small box from his drawer and pushed it across the desk.

"What's this?" He said nothing as I opened it, revealing a set of keys. My eyes widened. "Is this…"

He was beaming. "You need a car. It's your graduation present from Viola and me."

I didn't know what to say. No one had been as generous as these two, not even my parents...even when things were on good terms. I shook my head and put the box back on the desk. "I can't. It's too much."

"It's not too much," he said. "You're starting college in the fall, and you'll be coming and going. It makes sense for you to have your own car. You remember how to drive, right?"

When I'd first moved in, Charlie not only enrolled me in school and made my doctor and dentist appointments, he'd also signed me up for driving lessons. It had been a year since I'd driven, though. I knew I wasn't any good.

"I think so."

He led me out the front door, and there it was—a pearl white Honda Civic with a sunroof, shiny tires, and slightly tinted windows—to keep the sun off Hope's face, he explained. I opened the door and took in the black leather seats and new car smell. Everything about it seemed futuristic, from the push button ignition to the navigation system. There was even a sunroof, which I knew I'd use now that summer was here. A new car seat sat in the back, replacing the one Hope had almost outgrown. This one would transition to a booster seat when she was ready. It even had cup holders, which I thought was both adorably convenient and a gateway to future messes.

"It's perfect," I said, and I meant it. If I had picked out a car for myself, this would be the one.

"Want to test it out?"

I started to get in, then stopped.

"I need to say thank you to Viola, too," I said, moving back toward the house. Charlie stopped me with a shake of his head. I smiled sadly. She had no idea about the car. I knew this. In the past year, she'd slowly forgotten who I was, who Hope was, even who Charlie was. In the earlier days of her dementia, she'd been like my mother. But now, she no longer spoke, and seemed more like a child than an elderly woman.

"I know," I said to Charlie, without even needing to say what I knew. "But I owe her so much."

"You don't owe us anything," he said, his eyes intent as they met mine. "But you will if you wake her. Let her sleep, and go have a good time."

I smiled, getting into the driver's seat. I ran my hands over the smooth wheel. This was *my* car? Charlie hopped in the passenger seat. I teared up as I looked at him, and he squeezed my hand. I felt like Cinderella in a storybook life.

"It's too much," I said, but he shook his head. U

"You're worth this, and so much more."

I didn't believe him. He told me this all the time, but I had a hard time grasping the worth part. I didn't feel worthy; I felt lucky.

"Thank you so much. For this. For everything."

He shrugged as if giving me a brand new car was no big deal. "You're like a daughter to us. We just want you and Hope to have everything you need."

"We do," I assured him.

I slowly drove us down the gravel driveway onto the paved road. The butterflies in my stomach relaxed when I realized driving was like riding a bicycle—I hadn't forgotten how. The lessons I'd learned stuck with me as I merged into traffic, made left-hand turns, and cruised Petaluma's roads.

It was a short drive, but Charlie acted as if he were a tour guide, narrating every single landmark we passed.

"And to our right, we have the crooked tree that will soon take down those power lines if old Mr. Phillips doesn't get his act together and trim the branches." I giggled at Charlie's fake British accent as he went on roasting our neighbors as I drove by their houses. His silliness helped to take some of my jitters away. Still, I felt a bit nervous that I'd made some kind of mistake. A couple of times I pushed the brake too hard, and we both lurched forward as I came to a stop. If he noticed, though, he didn't say anything.

I turned on one of the cul-de-sacs and headed back toward our country road that led back to the house, then drove slowly up our gravel road. The house looked tiny against the vine-covered hillsides surrounding it, the red tile roof and cream walls a stark contrast to the green fields on all sides. I steered away from the circular driveway in front of the house and started to park near the work trucks, but Charlie stopped me, directing me toward the six-car garage.

"This one is yours," he said, pointing a clicker at the third stall. "This way, no crop dust will dirty the car." The door rose, but I didn't drive in right away. This seemed so unreal.

"What did I ever do to deserve this?"

He leaned over and kissed my forehead. "You were born."

I pulled into the garage carefully, taking way too long to get the car inside. I was afraid of scraping the sides or driving into the back of the garage, even though there was plenty of room to park.

Hope was playing in the front garden while Fátima pulled weeds among the lavender. She waved when she saw me, and then pointed in my direction to Hope. While Charlie went inside, I ran toward Fátima and Hope in the garden so I could gush about my new car. It turned out she knew, and had kept Charlie's secret.

"Want to go for a drive?" I asked her. Her face broke into a grin as she nodded.

"Let me go check on Señora Winston," she told me. "And then I go."

I carried Hope to the garage and buckled her into her car seat. She was oblivious to the expensive gift we'd just been given. But she *was* only two. I hoped I'd never get used to this. I didn't want to take any of it for granted.

With Fátima in the passenger seat and Hope humming in the back, we drove into town. I kept the sunroof open and the windows down, and our hair flew around our faces as the Foo Fighters blared from the speakers. I felt free, like we were flying down the road instead of driving. I could now go anywhere I wanted at any time without needing to coordinate with Charlie.

"Do you want to get coffee?" I asked. "There's a shop that serves up some of the best iced lattes around, and they have chocolate milk for Hope."

"Si," she said. "That sounds good."

I pulled into a parking spot in front of The Apple Box, a cute café next to the Petaluma River. As I was unbuckling Hope she looked at me, and I recognized the look of panic on her face.

"Do you need to go potty?" She nodded.

"I take her," Fátima said, pushing a $5 bill in my hand. I shook my head and handed it back, insisting I could pay. Once she gave me her order, they disappeared down the walkway and I headed into the café.

There were several reasons why I loved this coffee shop over all the others in Petaluma. For one, they played good music, but kept it low so you could actually hold a conversation, read, or just sit and do homework. Second, the outdoor deck seating offered a perfect view of the river, plus shade under oversized umbrellas. Third, the place was owned by a large Greek family who knew how to feed their customers. The menu changed every day, depending on the ingredients they had, but always with a Mediterranean theme. No one left this place hungry. Finally, they didn't just sell coffee here. As I entered the café, I paused to check out the latest knick-knacks they were selling on a few tables along the wall. Books, ceramics, magnets, postcards…all of them unique and made by local artists. I sometimes wondered if the creators were in the café, watching me as I scanned their creations.

"What can I get for you?" the guy at the cash register asked. I looked from the tables to him, and blushed when I saw the way he was looking at me. The front of his blonde hair was long enough to reach his eyes, and he shook his head to move it to the side. He gave me a dimpled grin, and I felt my cheeks get hot.

"What's good?" I asked, raising an eyebrow as I looked at his mouth. His smile deepened on one side, and I saw the interest in his face. I quickly looked away. He was undeniably cute, and I felt out of practice with flirting, dating, romance…

"All of it," he assured me. "But you'll definitely want to try the baklava. It's today's special."

"I'll take that, plus two iced lattes and a chocolate milk." He looked let down as he rang up my order. "Did I order the wrong thing?"

"Why do you ask?"

"You look disappointed."

"No," he said. "I didn't realize you were here with someone. I mean, sure you are. You're a pretty girl. But I'd hoped…" He trailed off.

"I don't have a boyfriend, if that's what you're saying." I didn't know where my boldness came from. I hadn't had a boyfriend since Jordan, and dating anyone else kind of freaked me out. But I'd also experienced jealousy in high school, watching other girls lead normal dating lives while I went home to Hope. Maybe it was the sudden freedom that came with the new car, or that I'd graduated and was no longer some high school girl.

"I'm Maddie," I told him, and reached my hand across the counter. He took my hand to shake it, but didn't let it go.

"I'm—"

"Maddie, lo siento," Fátima came up holding Hope. There was an unmistakable wet spot on her shirt, and I could see Hope's pants were soaked through. "We didn't make it in time." I felt the cashier's hand leave mine as my attention moved to my daughter.

"Mama," Hope whimpered, reaching out. I took her from Fátima, knowing my shirt was about to get wet, as well.

"Don't worry; mistakes happen," I told Hope. "We'll get you your chocolate milk and go home to change, okay?" She nodded, and burrowed her face in my shoulder. I turned back to the guy at the counter. "Sorry about that," I said, and paused. He didn't need to say anything else; his look said it all.

"Um, I'm just going to get your drinks ready."

"You were about to tell me your name," I reminded him. Maybe I was wrong. Maybe I'd caught him off guard.

He pointed to his nametag. Grayson.

"Did you want anything else?" he asked.

A normal life.

I felt ashamed as soon as I thought it. Was I really willing to trade in my role as Hope's mother for five minutes of flirting? I looked down at her, touching my forehead to hers. She put her hand on my cheek, and I could smell an unmistakable odor. I was pretty sure I now had pee on my face.

"Nope, that'll do it," I said.

In the five minutes it took for our drinks to hit the counter, Hope went from a wet toddler to a whiny pile of misery. I sensed her meltdown coming as Grayson set down her chocolate milk. I saw the irritation in his eyes. He wanted us gone. Hell, *I* wanted us gone. Just as Hope was about to let loose, I shoved the milk in her hands.

"Here, drink this," I instructed her, trying not to let frustration leak into my voice. Fátima took our iced coffees and the bagged dessert, and we headed for the door. As we left, I noticed a boy I'd gone to school with. I didn't know him very well, only that his name was Jace, and he was part of a popular group of guys who never gave someone like me the time of day. Today, though, his friends were nowhere around. He was sitting alone, a book in his hands and a half-eaten baklava in front of him. It looked like Grayson had talked him into today's special, too.

Jace looked at me with pity, his brow furrowed and his amber eyes concerned. Or maybe he was glaring. I couldn't tell. I felt like everyone was looking at me, the wet spot on my shirt, and the sniffling toddler in my arms sucking on her chocolate milk. I felt judged, as if they were wondering about the teen mom who didn't even know how to potty train her child. In five minutes, I'd made mistake after mistake—believing a guy might be interested in someone like me, quieting my child with a sugary drink, not getting her to the bathroom in time, not bringing a change of clothes… I'd been a parent almost three years, and even I wondered if I knew what I was doing.

"Hey," Jace said softly, but I pretended not to hear him. I felt tears burning in my eyes, and didn't want anyone to see me cry. I pushed past him and out the door, following Fátima to the car. I winced as I set Hope into the brand-new car seat, knowing it would probably smell like urine from now on.

I'm such an idiot.

Fátima tried to make light of things on the way home. I laughed at her jokes in an effort to hide my shame. I knew she saw through it, but played along as if everything was fine. By the time we reached home, Hope was asleep. The mostly empty cup lay on the leather seat, a pool of brown liquid underneath. *So much for cup holders.* I closed my eyes and breathed for a moment.

"I'll take her," Fátima said, but I waved her off.

"I've got her." I used my sleeve to wipe the seat, and picked up the cup. I didn't argue with Fátima when she took it from me and walked toward the house. Gingerly, I lifted Hope from the car seat and carried her into the house. I thought about letting her nap in her wet clothes, but only for a moment. If I did, I knew her sensitive skin would break out into a rash. I carried her to my room, put a towel on the bed, and set her down.

"Hope, honey, wake up," I coaxed, moving her gently as she stretched in her sleep. She opened her eyes and frowned, irritated by the interruption. "You're wet," I explained. "Let's get you into the bath." She reached her hand down and touched her wet pants. Her lower lip pushed out as she looked at me.

"I sorry, Mama," she whimpered, but I shook my head.

"Don't worry about it," I told her as I took off her wet pants. "It was only an accident."

I turned on the hot water in the tub, holding her wrapped up in a towel in my lap as the water warmed. Once it reached the right temperature, I placed her in the tub and added bubbles underneath the running water. The water foamed up beneath the spout, spreading throughout the water and underneath Hope's clapping hands. She hit the water and bubbles flew everywhere.

"Hold on." I laughed and put her toy boats in the water. As she carved trails through the bubbles with the boats, I changed out of my wet shirt, watching her through the doorway.

"Mama, you take bath, too?"

"No baby, I'll take one later," I told her, returning to the bathroom and sitting on the closed toilet seat. I put my hands in the warm water, and we played for another fifteen minutes. She yawned several times, and I hoped she might still take a nap. I was tired, too.

"Ready?" I asked. She nodded and stood up in the tub, her arms over her head. I pulled the plug, and the water gurgled as it made its way down the drain. I took a fresh towel and picked her up with it. In my room, she helped me pull the shirt over her head and put her pants on.

"I sleep here?" she asked. I thought it over, then nodded. "You too, Mama," she said, patting the bed next to her when I placed her between the covers. I smiled. I loved times like these, just the two of us snuggling together.

"Me, too," I agreed, and slipped under the covers with her. She curled into me as I wrapped my arms around her. She smelled of lavender and vanilla, the scent of her bath bubbles.

At first, she wouldn't stop fidgeting. She rolled against me, then away, then back again. I realized she was playing, and clicked my tongue at her. She got the message and lay still. I could hear her humming as my mind grew heavy. Soon her little chest began moving up and down with each breath, her eyes closed and mouth open as she slept. I stared at her for a moment, drinking in her perfect features and delicate fingers next to her mouth. She would be three in a few months, but I still had moments when I couldn't believe she was mine.

I leaned over and brushed my lips against her forehead, holding my breath so she'd stay asleep. "I love you, Hope," I whispered. She sighed and continued sleeping.

The Gardener

On Saturday, Charlie gave me a day off from working the vineyard so I could sleep in and have a normal summer day like a regular teen on summer break—except not every teen had his or her own mini-alarm clock. I awoke to Hope slamming her upper body against my bed as she tried to climb up.

"What are you doing?" I groaned, peering through heavy lids at my toddler as she continued to try to reach me. I pulled her up the rest of the way and hugged her. "How did you get out of your crib?"

"I climb, Mama," she said, and I could hear the pride in her voice. I had visions of her falling off the rail and cracking her head open. She was obviously ready for a toddler bed. But was I ready for that step? With no barriers, I knew I'd get many early mornings with my energetic girl. I looked at the clock on my bedside table. 5:43 a.m.

"Baby, the sun hasn't even come up. It's still nighttime, time to sleep."

"I sleep with you, Mama," she insisted, pushing herself harder against me. I sighed into her hair, but felt too tired to argue.

"Okay, but you have to sleep for real," I told her.

To her credit, she tried really hard, lying against me as she hummed and played with the sheet. Each time she plucked the fabric, it vibrated the bed just enough to keep me from sleep. When that didn't entertain her, she rolled over and played with my face.

"Baby, I'm sleeping," I told her. She didn't say anything, but I felt her breath against my cheeks. I opened my eyes and found her staring at me.

"You awake now, Mama?" I closed my eyes again and sighed.

"No," I moaned. "Can't you sleep?"

"I get up," she said. Before I could argue, she slipped off the side of the bed and padded to the door. I heard her nudge it open, then close it. Groaning, I forced myself to sit up and wipe the sleep from my eyes. If she was up, I had to be up. I could only imagine what she'd get into on her own in this huge house.

I found her pulling toys from the bin in the living room. The lucky girl had something to play with in every room of the house, thanks in part to me, but mostly because Charlie seemed to bring something new home for her every week. She had more toys than she could play with.

When she saw me, she got up and threw herself at my knees. Looking up, she frowned. "I'm hungry," she whined.

"Of course you are." I picked her up, carried her to the kitchen, and set her in the booster seat on her chair. "Do you want cereal?" She shook her head. "Toast with jam?" Again, it was a no. "How about scrambled eggs?"

"No Mama." Her lips pushed out in a pout.

"Well, what *do* you want, then?"

"Pork chops." I stared at her. Last week when we had pork chops for dinner, she wouldn't even eat them when I added some ketchup to her plate. I ended up making her a bowl of spaghetti while the rest of us ate the dinner Fátima had made.

"We don't have any pork chops," I told her. Hope's lip pushed out even more, and her eyes narrowed.

"I want pork chops!" she insisted, each word louder than the last.

"Shhh, Hope! Everyone's asleep." I glanced at the clock. It was just past 6 a.m. I opened the refrigerator, hoping to find a pork chop had miraculously appeared. There was none. But there was a plate of chicken from last night's dinner.

"Pork chops it is." I pulled the chicken out and heated it in the microwave. Then I cut it into bite-size pieces, added some ketchup to her plate, and set it in front of her. "Here you go, princess," I told her. "Delicious, not-for-breakfast pork chops."

She looked at the plate for a second, moving the food around with her fork. Then she clumsily speared one and put it in her mouth. Her face lit up.

"I like pork chops!" she said, her mouth full. I refrained from rolling my eyes, and just nodded.

"Yup, tastes like chicken, huh?"

"NO Mama, not chicken. Pork chops."

"Whatever," I muttered, but couldn't help laughing at both her stubbornness and my cleverness.

It was Fátima's day off, so it was my responsibility to make sure Viola was up and dressed. When the sun began to shine through the window blinds, I crept over to her room and peeked in. She was awake, eyes open as she stared toward the window.

"Good morning, Viola," I murmured, easing into her room so I wouldn't startle her. She turned to me, a look of surprise on her face. I paused, resting my hand on the foot of her bed. We'd learned to move slowly, talk slowly, even think slowly around her. We were strangers to her, and any sudden movement might mean a bad day for all of us.

It hadn't always been this way. When I first met her, Viola was just beginning to show signs of dementia, but she still carried herself with almost a regal air. I was homeless when we first met. She and Charlie had pulled into the parking lot where I lived, and she'd leaned across him from her passenger seat, calling out to me as I waited with other workers looking for a job. She'd appeared delicate back then, just as she did now, but the difference was in her conduct. Even hidden under large sunglasses and a hat, I could sense she was a woman with a mission. I'd soon learn this to be true, though she approached everything with a gentle touch. She'd hired me as their housekeeper, trusting me with the care of their large vineyard home. I'd just been grateful for the much-needed money it put in my pocket, and had no idea they hired me because they could see I needed help. I reminded them of their daughter, they later told me—a girl who reached a tragic end when mistaken for an intruder in their house. I was their path toward redemption. They were my second chance at life. We saved each other.

I was willing to do anything for this woman. Now that she required so much care, I was happy to help.

"Good morning," I repeated, offering her a warm smile. Her weathered face mirrored my smile, and I relaxed. "Are you ready to get up?" I didn't expect her to say anything. Sometimes I wondered if she even understood me. She didn't seem to have a problem when I took her hands in mine, and she hummed as I sat her at the edge of the bed, her long nightgown covering her legs and her bare feet swinging just above the floor. It seemed today was going to be one of her good days.

Hope came into the room, and Viola turned from me to watch my little girl grab the blocks from the basket in the corner. I took advantage of the distraction to help Viola undress. She didn't fight me as I put a robe on her and led her to the bathroom. She only had eyes for Hope. Once undressed and in the tub, however, she closed her eyes and let me pour warm water over her long, white hair. I positioned myself so I could take care of her while also able to see Hope playing, who was busy sorting her blocks by colors. I added a few drops of tear-free shampoo to Viola's hair, and she stayed still like a well-behaved child. A few times, she looked at me and smiled. She said nothing, even as I rambled on about what Charlie was teaching me, the things Hope and I did during the week, and what our plans were for the day. I talked just to fill the silence, wondering what I sounded like to her. She seemed happy, however, which I took to be a good thing. Maybe that was all that mattered—that she was happy.

Following Viola's bath, I held her arm as she stepped carefully onto the mat, then dried her with a big, fluffy towel. Now that she was comfortable with me, she lost all sense of caution or modesty. She stood naked in front of me, unembarrassed, lifting her arms so I could dry her upper body and help her into her robe. Each day I tried to guess her mental age. Today she seemed five, and I raised an eyebrow as I watched her focus on Hope. I could almost feel her longing to join my daughter on the ground with the piles of colorful blocks.

"Did you want to play, Viola?" I asked her. She looked at me. She didn't answer, but I saw her eyes light up. I smiled at this moment of clarity. I quickly dressed her, then combed out her long hair and braided it. "We'll play out on the back porch," I told her. "It's too beautiful to stay inside."

She let me lead her to the covered porch that looked out on the garden she once worked in. Beyond the overgrown flowers was a hillside covered in vines. It had become one of my favorite spots to read, though seeing the garden now reminded me how much I'd neglected it.

"Wait here while I get Hope and the blocks," I told her once she had settled in her chair.

Hope helped me carry the blocks outside—meaning she carried one in each hand and I carried the rest in the basket. I gently scattered them on the table near Viola, and the two of them took turns placing the blocks in appropriate piles. Even though Viola didn't say a word, it was as if they spoke the same language. I watched as Viola gestured to a block across the table. Hope didn't hesitate to pick it up and place it in Viola's hand. They played silently like this for a while, and I sat nearby to rest. I wanted to nod off for a few minutes to catch up on the sleep I missed, but the weeds in front of me were too distracting. They'd grown as tall as the flowers; I saw them even with my eyes closed, and I finally gave up on my catnap. Hope and Viola were still engrossed in their block project, so it was a good time to tend to the garden.

By the back door was a bucket of garden supplies that hadn't been moved in months. I brushed away the spider webs on top and pulled out the gardening gloves and kneepad. I placed the pad on the ground. Then, with gloves on, I started pulling the weeds by the roots until there was a pile next to me. I kept looking over to the "girls," checking to make sure they were still playing. Viola looked tired, yet still focused on what she was doing. They'd built a tower together. As soon as it was tall enough, Hope knocked it over and they both giggled. Then Hope scrambled to pick up the blocks so they could rebuild.

There were more weeds than I could pull in one day, but I was pleased when I saw the progress I'd made in the one area. I moved to another part of the garden, bare except for the weeds. There was enough space to plant vegetables, I was sure. I grabbed a shovel and started to tackle the weeds by digging them out, but stopped when I saw Viola's head sleepily nodding.

"Time to go inside," I called, wiping my forehead and leaning the shovel next to the fence.

Hope got down from her seat while Viola stared out at the garden. She pointed, and I looked where she was gesturing.

"Bird." Her whisper was so soft I barely heard it. Sure enough, there was a hummingbird flicking its beak in one of the foxgloves.

"That's right," I said, smiling in pleasure. She spoke!

I led her into the house and made her a bowl of soup, cooling it with an ice cube. Beside her, Hope ate a peanut butter and jelly sandwich. I ate a hybrid of the two, enjoying the savory broth with the sweet sandwich. When we were finished, I placed Hope in her playpen in the living room, then led Viola to her room and helped her into bed. She looked at me and patted my hand.

"Bird," she whispered, closing her eyes.

Charlie's office door was ajar, and I could see him working on something. I knocked and he locked up.

"Hey Maddie," he said as I pushed the door open.

"Hey," I said back. "Did you know Viola still talks?"

He raised his eyebrows. "What did she say?"

"Nothing much," I admitted. "She saw a hummingbird and said 'bird.' Then she said it again when I helped her to bed."

"Well, isn't that something," he said, leaning back in his chair and smiling as I had. "Sometimes I think she hears me when I'm talking to her." His smile faded, and he turned his gaze to the window. "I've wondered if I'd ever hear her voice again."

I'd often thought about what it must be like for Charlie. He loved Viola so much. From the first day I met them, he took special care of her—opening doors for her, making sure she was happy, protecting her from memories she'd rather forget.... Now in the middle of her dementia, he made sure she was always comfortable, and spent many hours with her. They no longer slept in the same bed; since Viola often didn't remember who he was, it would be alarming for her to wake up next to a "stranger." But he spent every evening in her room, watching TV with her from a chair next to her bed while she nodded off to sleep.

I understood falling in love, but had a hard time grasping how this one-sided love could be enough.

"How's she doing today?" Charlie's question brought me back to the present.

"She and Hope had a good time building block towers," I said, smiling as I recalled the morning. He gave a light laugh as he nodded.

"Hope is good for her."

"They're good for *each other*," I corrected. "Those two, it's like they're both…" I trailed off, realizing I was talking about Charlie's wife.

"Toddlers," he finished for me. I winced, but he shook his head. "It's okay," he told me. "It's true. I love Viola with all my heart. I often think of the day we got married, and the wonderful romance we've shared over the years. We grew up together, raised a family together, and got old together. She still looks like the woman I love, and she still holds many of the qualities I've always loved about her. But now, instead of just loving her as her husband, I also love her as if I were her father. She needs care more than ever, and I'll do anything to make sure she gets it."

"I hope one day I'm loved that way."

He smiled, but I saw the sadness in his face.

"I hope you *never* have to be cared for that way."

I understood what he meant. I knew he loved Viola, but I also knew he was exhausted. However, I couldn't help but think that Viola got the better end of the deal. She might not remember, and she might require constant care.

It was a lot of work on all our parts, and I knew Charlie missed his wife. But she was happy. Forgetting didn't seem like the worst thing in the world.

"How did you two meet?" I asked. Charlie sat back in his chair as he thought back to the past.

"We were just kids then," he said. "My family had moved from Kentucky to Montana when I was fifteen, and I didn't know a lot of people, especially girls. I went to an all-boys school, and Viola went to the all-girls one across town. The only time we got to meet any girls was at the school dances, which they held three times each year." He stopped, and then laughed. "It wasn't exactly love at first sight. She was way out of my league, and I had no idea how to even get someone like her interested in me. Plus, I already knew this other guy, Billy Weston, was interested in her, and they'd been on a few dates. But I was persistent. I'd find out from mutual friends where she would be, and I'd make sure I'd be there. We eventually became friends, but I still couldn't figure out how to get further with our relationship. She'd go out with Billy, they'd have some kind of fight, and then she'd meet up with me and cry over how much he frustrated her."

An amused look crossed Charlie's face, and he drummed the desk. "After hearing her complain about Billy for probably the twentieth time, I finally had enough. I told her, 'Viola, are you done messing around with this other guy, or what? I'm here, I love you, and I'll spend my whole life making you happy.'" Charlie laughed, and I could just see a younger version of him saying this to Viola. "Her eyes got really big," he continued. "Seems she really had no idea how I felt about her. But then she turned around and surprised me. She dropped Billy immediately, and we've been together ever since."

"So, how did you propose?" I asked.

"Nothing showy, like nowadays. There wasn't a crowd of people, a band, or anything like that. It was just the two of us, sitting in our favorite restaurant, and one tiny little ring, since that's all I could afford. We got married in the courthouse, with our parents and closest friends as witnesses. Then we moved into my uncle's house there in Montana, and began to make plans for our future."

"Which was buying a vineyard in California," I said.

"That's right," he said.

"But why a vineyard?"

"I guess it was a romantic idea," he said. "Viola's ancestors had been vintners in Italy. I think she wanted a way to feel close to her roots. I was just interested in making her happy. If she wanted a vineyard, I was going to get her a vineyard. I learned everything I could about growing grapes, maintaining the land, harvest, bottling, running a business... I spent years working the harvest at this one Montana vineyard, and got close enough to the owner that he trained me to be their winemaker. I saved everything I earned, socking it away for our future home. I dreamed of winters without snow, living near the ocean, owning my own home, and making my wife's dreams come true."

"And then you bought Winston Family Wines," I said.

"Except it wasn't Winston Family Wines then. It was a plot of land with a shack for a house. Viola and I moved in, and you'd think it was the Taj Majal the way she made such a fuss about it. Truly, you'd have been shocked if you'd seen how tiny and run down this place was. But she didn't care, and neither did I. We had our land, and we were closer to our dream. It took years, of course, but after putting in a lot of grunt work, we found our calling. It started out with just selling our grapes to other wineries until we had enough money to start bottling our own. We grew more vines, increased our bottlings, and built a new home on the property." He paused, looking at me. "And here we are now," he said.

"Here we are now," I agreed. He looked out the window, and then turned back to me

"All right, enough chatter. It's a nice day out. What are your plans?" he asked.

"Well, I was weeding the garden and noticed there's enough room to plant a few things. It's the perfect time of year to put in beets, carrots and squash, so I thought I'd take Hope with me to the Seed Bank and grab some seeds and see if they have any heirloom tomato starts."

"That will be a nice addition to Viola's garden," he said.

"I'm not the best with flowers, but I seem to have luck with vegetables. Not sure if it's me, or if they're just hardier plants, but they don't die on me. Plus, food tastes better out of the garden, don't you think?"

"Absolutely," he agreed. "I can't wait to taste what you grow."

With Charlie there with Viola, I grabbed Hope, a diaper bag with a change of clothes (just in case!), and my purse, and headed out the door. I opened the garage door with the clicker in my purse, and there was my white Honda looking back at me, ready to be driven. A few days had passed since I'd driven with Fátima, and this would be the first time driving without another adult in the car. I opened the door, enjoying the new car smell plus laundry detergent from Hope's freshly washed car seat cover. The urine smell seemed to have washed out just fine, and the seat looked as new as it did the first time I drove it.

"Ready to get some seeds?" I asked. Hope nodded, though I was pretty sure she had no idea what seeds were. I buckled her in and placed the bag on the floor, then took the stroller near the garage wall and stuck it in the trunk. Once in the car, I fiddled with the radio, programming in all my favorite stations. Then I scanned the stations until I landed on a Coldplay song, my favorite band of the moment. With the windows down and the radio up, we were off. I could hear Hope singing along in the back seat, her little voice joining the band as they sang about a sky full of stars. I sang with her, bringing the stars down from the sky and all around us as we drove beside vineyards and country roads on our way into town.

It took about fifteen minutes to reach downtown Petaluma. I felt nervous as I drove, adjusting my speed so I wasn't driving too slowly. When I reached the left turn toward the parking lot, my throat felt tight. I was sure the cars waiting behind me had seen a handful of times I could have turned, but didn't. I kept looking in the rearview mirror, clenching and unclenching my hands, thinking about the invisible car that would come out of nowhere and take out Hope and me. I was being ridiculous. At least nobody honked at me. I finally made the turn, letting out the air I'd been holding in as I searched for a parking spot away from other cars. I ended up on top of the parking structure, meaning I'd have to walk down the flight of stairs. Still, it was better than swiping any cars with my novice parking skills.

I'd put Hope in her stroller before I realized this wasn't going to work. I could carry the stroller down the stairs a step at a time or I could walk around and down the ramps until I reached the bottom. I looked at Hope, who seemed content playing with the belt around her waist.

"Let's go for a walk," I told her, and started toward the ramp. It was wide enough to accommodate pedestrians and vehicles, but I held my breath every time we came to a blind turn. I went wide at each turn to be sure cars would see us.

The walk to the Seed Bank was our reward. We passed quaint antique shops and cafés before reaching the historic corner building. In the 1920s, it had been a bank for money, not seeds, and the airy space still had that bank feel. It was both strange and expected that this large granite building with its classic marble and brass interior now held traditional and rare seeds of every variety, gardening tools and gifts, and displays of knickknacks that appealed to any gardener. While I wouldn't call myself an avid gardener, I'd learned to appreciate the trade after being around the vineyard for the past three years.

Tomato starts lined the sidewalk outside the building, and I looked them over. They were healthy plants, and I could almost taste the tomatoes as I inhaled their distinctive scent. I chose a few Beefsteak varieties, which would produce large, heavy tomatoes, and Black Russians for their rich taste and intriguing dark fruit. I rested them on the top of the stroller, and then entered the store.

"Let me know if I can help you find anything," the clerk called from the other side of the store. I nodded with a smile. I cruised Hope slowly down the row, studying the various seeds neatly lined up.

"So, which one of you is the gardener?" a voice asked, and I turned to see who it was. *Jace.* He was standing there so casual, as if we'd been friends in school. Thing is, we weren't. I didn't know him, and he sure as hell didn't know me. Yet, he was smiling at me as if I could be charmed by him—as if I was like every other girl who idolized the guys in his group. Sure, he was cute, especially with the way he had this tousled thing going on with his dark hair, and how his eyes were almost the color of honey…similar to mine and Hope's. I hated to admit it, but he even had an approachable air to him, and I was tempted to let go of my prejudices and be friendly back. Almost. He was one of the popular guys, and I was an outcast. I wasn't about to be made a fool of.

I gave him a half-smile, ready to turn and leave when he leapt passed me.

"Kayci, wait, put that down," he said, rescuing a potted plant from the hands of a little girl. The toddler burst into tears, reaching out as Jace took the plant away, then picked her up and soothed her, bouncing her a little as he wiped her hands. "That's not for you, baby," he said, kissing her on the forehead. She leaned into him and rested her head under his chin. He walked back to me, rolling his eyes. "Well, so much for my cool intro." He laughed. "Can we start over?"

"I'm the gardener," I said, relaxing a little as I looked at him curiously. "Hope hasn't done much gardening, but I have a feeling she's really going to love digging in the dirt like your daughter."

"Oh, she's not mine," he corrected me. "She's my baby sister. Hope is yours? Like, your *daughter?*" Once again, my cheeks burned. I looked at my feet a moment, embarrassed. *Really, Maddie? Is seeming cool to someone you barely know more important than Hope?*

"Yup," I looked boldly into his eyes. "She's mine. She'll be three in October." I waited for his face to change, for him to turn and make any kind of excuse to get far away from me. Instead, he balanced his sister on his hip and leaned down until they were eye level with Hope.

"Hey there," he said. Hope, lacking any self-consciousness, reached toward Kayci's golden curls. Kayci laughed and grabbed Hope's hand. "What's your name?" Jace asked Hope. She ignored him, too intent on the little girl in his arms.

"That's Hope," I told him. "And I'm Maddie. Maddie Russo."

He stood up and got ready to hold his hand out, but Kayci squirmed, trying to reach her new friend.

"I'm Jace Reynolds," he said, maneuvering the fidgeting girl until he could place her on the ground. She rushed to Hope's stroller and they took turns entertaining each other.

"I know," I said, and then rolled my eyes at how stupid and creepy that sounded. "I mean, we had a class together junior year, and I remember you from then."

"We did? How do I not remember you?"

"I was pretty new to school back then," I told him. "And I was kind of shy because I didn't know anyone, and because, well…" I looked down at Hope. I'd waited until she was almost one before I re-entered high school, making me a full year older than my classmates. I was pretty sure when I entered that no one else had a kid. I was right, at least not in the traditional part of our school. Other teen moms went to the continuation high school at the edge of campus. I didn't want to go there, so I tried to hide the fact that I had a baby. Of course, secrets never stay secret in high school. It was only a few weeks until the whispers started. Not everyone knew about Hope, but those who did stayed clear of me—as if teen pregnancy were contagious. I graduated without any close friends.

"I'm sorry I never knew you," he said. "I wish I had."

"Trust me, you're probably better off. Your reputation would have taken a hit." I wanted to pull the words back in as soon as I said them.

"My reputation?" He laughed and started to say something else, but a woman called his name from the front door. "My mom," he said reluctantly. "We're not done with this conversation," he went on with a smile. "What do you say to a playdate with the girls? Lucchesi Park, tomorrow at three?"

Wanting to say no, I nodded my head yes. *What is wrong with me?*

"Great, it's a date," he said with a wink. He was gone before I could even interpret what that meant.

The Playdate

Jace Reynolds.

I'd barely known him in school, and had never talked to him before we graduated. It was surprising I even remembered his name. Well, no. It would have been more surprising if he remembered mine. While he wasn't the most popular kid in school, he was well-liked, one of the elite. In our junior year, he sat toward the back of the classroom in the section that never wanted to be called on. Naturally, the teacher made it a point to call on that section as much as possible. I knew how things went, so I chose a seat in the middle of the class, and everyone ignored me most of the year. *Of course* Jace didn't remember me. I was invisible.

I barely thought about Jace while we were in school, so it seemed strange that I couldn't stop thinking about him since meeting him at the Seed Bank. I wasn't infatuated; I was confused. Why did a guy like Jace hang out with his toddler sister and mom at a seed store instead of with friends? Why didn't he back off when he found out I had a daughter? Was it stupid to agree to a playdate? Was I setting myself up to be the butt of some huge joke? What did he even want?

I thought about him all morning long while working with Charlie in the vineyards, tying back branches and thinning vines. The questions rolled through my head as I dug in the garden with Hope in the early afternoon. And as the clock moved closer to 3 p.m., butterflies performed figure eights in my stomach. I even considered not showing up. After all, he didn't have my phone number or know where I lived. I could disappear and he'd forget me.

I told myself this, even as I showered off the dirt and dressed Hope in a clean outfit. I thought about things I could do instead of going to the park as I applied mascara and lip gloss. I considered turning down random side streets as I drove us to the park. And as I strapped Hope into her stroller and made my way toward the playground, I kept telling myself I could turn around and walk away. But as soon as I could see the park and Jace pushing his sister on the swings, I stopped pretending. I lit up when he waved at me, though I was still nervous.

"Don't make me a fool," I whispered, giving him a small smile and rolling Hope to the edge of the sand. I unstrapped her and carried her to the swings, placing her in the one next to Kayci.

"Hey." Jace gave me a sideways grin.

"Hey." I was overthinking everything, and then I began to overthink my overthinking. *What is my problem?*

We pushed the girls in awkward silence, and once again I started second-guessing my decision to come. I didn't even know what I was thinking. It was weird to be in a park with a guy who could bowl me over with his social standing, pushing my daughter and his sister on the swings as if this were a normal thing. It *wasn't* normal. If his friends knew he was here with me, I wondered what they'd say. I imagined it wouldn't be anything nice. The thought jabbed at me, but when I turned to ask what his motives were, he finally spoke.

"There's a sandbox over there for little kids, if you want to take the girls over," he said. "Can you take Kayci? I'll be right back." I didn't know what to say as he pulled her from the swing. The realization hit me as I lifted Hope. I took Kayci's hand and headed toward the sandbox. By the time I reached it, I was furious. He didn't want a playdate. He wanted a babysitter for his sister. I should have known better.

It was almost ten minutes before he came back. The girls were digging in the sand, laughing. I hated to break this budding friendship up, especially since Hope never played with any other kids. But I'd be damned if I stuck around and let this guy make an idiot of me.

"Thanks for watching the girls," he said, but then paused when he saw me glaring at him. "What's wrong?" he asked, shrugging off his backpack.

"What's *wrong*?" I repeated. "What's wrong is that I even agreed to come here. I should have stayed home. Just because I'm a mom doesn't mean I'm free to watch your sister while you take off and do whatev… What's that?"

"A soda," he said, holding a can toward me. "And there's snacks, too. Kayci was too excited to get to the park that I had to leave them in the cooler in my trunk. I thought we might enjoy something to eat while we're here."

"Oh." My cheeks were on fire.

"I'm sorry I made you watch Kayci. I didn't want to take her all the way back to the car. I won't do it again."

"No! It was my mistake," I said. "I thought you were going off to hang with friends or something and just needed me to watch your sister."

"Wow," he said, shaking his head and rubbing the back of his neck.

"I know. I'm sorry."

"No, it's brilliant. I should have thought of that first." I rolled my eyes as he grinned. "Maddie, I would never do that."

"So, food, huh?" I said, changing the subject. He opened his backpack wider and threw me a package of fruit snacks.

"They're the fancy kind," he said as I raised an eyebrow, "shaped like the fruit they're supposed to taste like."

"I love fruit snacks," I admitted.

"Right? How can you not?"

I ate a few jellied pieces, and put one in Hope's mouth so her sandy fingers wouldn't get on the sticky snacks. She took a few, but was so busy playing with Kayci I ended up eating the rest of the bag.

"Tell me about this reputation I seem to have," Jace said. Once again, my cheeks started to flush.

"That was stupid to say," I told him. "I don't even know you."

"You seem to know enough."

"I didn't mean it," I insisted. "I just—"

"I'm not mad, Maddie. I just want to know how you see me."

I paused before answering. How *did* I see him? I realized I didn't know him at all. I knew who he hung out with at school, but I couldn't name his best friend. I didn't know his favorite music or what he liked to do on the weekend. I couldn't read what he was thinking while he watched me, a smile on his face, waiting for me to answer.

"I guess it has more to do with how I see *me*," I finally admitted. He raised an eyebrow. The statement hung between us for a moment while we watched the girls. Hope had lifted a handful of sand and let it trickle down on Kayci's head. I started to get up and put an end to it, but Jace stopped me.

"They're fine," he said. "If Kayci didn't like it, she'd do something about it." Sure enough, Kayci was laughing as the sand fell through her hair. "That'll be fun to clean up," he said.

I looked at him, confused. He was eighteen years old, on his summer vacation, and had the freedom to do anything he wanted. Yet, he was here with his toddler sister at the park.

"What?" Jace asked. I realized I was staring and quickly looked away.

"I don't understand," I said. "You could be doing anything right now. Hanging out with friends. Sleeping all day. Doing whatever normal people our age do. But instead, you're here with me, watching a couple of toddlers. The way you talk, it's like you do this all the time."

"That's probably because I do." He looked over at Kayci and smiled. Then he looked back at me. "Or maybe it's just an excuse to hang out with you." I rolled my eyes at this as he gave me a lopsided grin.

"So, you use your little sister as bait?" I said with a smirk. "Man, Reynolds, your game needs some serious work."

He laughed at this and shook his head.

"Why though?" I continued. "I mean, don't get me wrong. I love playing with my daughter. She's a lot of fun. But this is my world now, and she's a part of me. If I weren't a mom, I'd be doing anything but this. I'd go to the movies. I'd take naps every afternoon, stay up late, sleep in every morning. I'd work at some dumb job to save money so I could spend it on stupid stuff like makeup or going out to eat instead of toddler toys, little kid movies, and craft supplies to keep her occupied. And I definitely wouldn't be hanging out in a park with a toddler."

I could hardly remember what life was like before having a kid. What the heck did I do with all my time? Now, I felt like I was *on* every moment—probably because I was.

"I still do all that stuff," he said. "But the thing is, my mom works, and it's easier if I watch Kayci instead of some stranger. Plus, I like hanging out with her. She's hilarious. Here, watch this." He turned toward Kayci and started singing the first few lines of "Can't Stop the Feeling" in a perfect Justin Timberlake impression. As soon as he got to the chorus, she started dancing before collapsing in a ball of laughter on the sand. He scooped her up and buried his face in her belly while she laughed harder.

"Seriously," he said with a grin after he put her down. "You can't even train dogs to be this cool. Ugh, I think I have sand in my mouth." He wiped at his mouth while I giggled.

The short attention span of the girls meant we were unable to have any kind of deep conversation. I not only expected this, I felt relieved by it. Since finding out I was pregnant, my social life pretty much ended. I'd forgotten what it was like to hang out with people my own age outside of school. Keeping the focus of this "date," or whatever it was supposed to be, as a playdate for the girls took a lot of the pressure off—though it didn't stop me from overthinking the whole thing.

Is this a date? Or is this just a guy looking to make friends for his little sister?

"Jace, dere!" Kayci called, rushing over to grab Jace's hand and pull him toward the swings. Hope laughed and ran to me, ready to copy everything her new friend was doing.

"Dere, Mama," she urged, holding my hand and swinging it. I was pretty sure she didn't know what "dere" was.

"All right, you two," Jace said, laughing. He pretended Kayci was pulling him up, then swung her in his arms. "Come on, Kayci, let's go," he said as she squealed.

"Let's go, KK," Hope said, lifting her arms to me so I could pick her up, too.

"That's cute. KK," Jace repeated. He looked at Kayci. "You want to swing, KK?" he asked her.

"Yes!" We took the girls to neighboring swings and put them in the baskets. I could tell Kayci was a little more fearless than Hope as Jace pulled her swing back and let her fly fast. The look on her face was one of pure glee, and she tilted her head back and laughed. "More!" she cried.

Hope had always been cautious, from playing on the playground to walking up and down the stairs holding my hand. So I didn't even try to keep up with Jace and Kayci. I pushed Hope lightly, and she threw her head back and laughed as if she were swinging as high as Kayci. I giggled at my little copycat, amused by how much she idolized her new friend.

Kayci seemed to know the playground well. We were only at the swings for five minutes before she was ready to get down and go to something new. Jace lifted her and set her on the ground, and she started to run toward the play structure but then stopped and turned around.

"Come on, girl," she said to Hope, holding out her hand.

"That's Hope," Jace said.

"Come on, girl Hope," Kayci said.

Hope squirmed to get out of her seat. "Mama, help!" she said. I lifted her up, and then set her on the ground. She ran to Kayci, who took her hand and pulled her to the structure.

"Kayci, slow down, she's little," Jace called. We walked after them as Kayci climbed the stairs and Hope struggled to follow. I helped her, then let Kayci lead her to the top.

"Hi Mama," Hope called through the tube, looking down at me.

This part of the playground was a hit. Both girls took turns going up the structure and sliding down the slide. Hope seemed to get faster with each run up the stairs, and soon refused my assistance as she teetered her way up. I stood by, just in case.

"They're having a lot of fun," Jace said next to me. I nodded, looking over at him. "But it doesn't make it easy to talk, does it?"

"Not really," I said, and wrinkled my nose. "These two are all over the place." They were now back in the sand,

Kayci digging a hole. I could tell by the look on Hope's face that she was fighting off tiredness. We'd have to leave soon if I wanted to avoid any meltdowns.

"What do you say we go out sometime again, but this time without the kids?"

Again, I wondered what this meant. *Is he looking for a friendly hangout, and that's it? Or is he looking for something more?*

"I'd love to," I told him. "I'm good most evenings, especially if we time it after Hope's bedtime. She's usually asleep by 7."

Am I interested in this going any further than friendship? Could he be someone I'd be happy with? How will Hope be around him if we start seeing each other more?

"How about tomorrow night, then? I can pick you up at 7:30."

That would make three days in a row I'd seen him, counting the brief time in the Seed Bank. That had to mean something, right?

"That's perfect."

"Great! It's a date," he said, like he did the first day. He said it so casually, as if a "date" could be watching football with the boys or going shopping with his mom. Maybe that was all the meaning this would have. Maybe. But then, it was three days in a row, and he wanted to hang out in the evening.

What does it all mean?

He nudged me with his shoulder. "Hey, what's going on?"

I shook my head. "Nothing, why?"

"You seem really serious. What are you thinking?"

If I'm heading into something I'm not ready for. If I'm about to make a total fool of myself. If I'm ready to open myself up to friendship, maybe even more. If I... If I'm even worthy of having a guy like you interested in a girl like me.

"No, really. Nothing." He raised his eyebrow. "Okay, fine," I said. "I'm thinking about how much fun I'm having here today with you, but I'm also looking at the time. It's almost Hope's naptime." I glanced at her; she was rubbing her face. I winced as she got sand in her eyes and saw the meltdown before it even happened. "Like clockwork," I said as she broke out into a wail.

We walked over to the girls and scooped them up. I poured some water from my bottle on her eye, and she acted as if I were drowning her.

"I just need to get the sand out, sweetie," I said. She wasn't having it, but I insisted. Once it was over, she sniffled into my shoulder as if I'd wounded her.

"Tomorrow we go to the park, Jace?" Kayci asked. Her verbal skills surprised me. She was only a little older than Hope, but seemed so much more advanced. Hope had only started talking in two- or three-word sentences over the past few months. Kayci, on the other hand, was holding full conversations.

"I have to work, and then Maddie and I are going to hang out," he told her. She frowned at him. "But maybe the next day?" Just like that, her smile was back.

He walked me back to my car, even though his was down the street. I scribbled directions to my house on the back of a receipt and handed it to him before I threw the diaper bag in the car.

"Give me your phone," he said as I started to get Hope out of the stroller. I handed it to him, and he shifted Kayci in his arms so he could type. Once Hope was buckled into her car seat, he handed my phone back to me.

"I put my contact information in your phone, and then I sent myself a text from your phone so I have your information, too." He looked at his phone and smirked. "That's really nice of you to say."

I narrowed my eyes at him, biting back a grin. Then I opened my texts and read the message "I" sent him.

Me: *I had a really great time with you today. BTW, I think you're pretty hot.*

I started to laugh, and then saw the three dots at the bottom of the message, indicating he was typing. Then the message pushed through.

Jace: *Why, thank you! I think I can honestly say you're the prettiest girl I've ever met.*

My face burned as I read his words. I looked back up at him, and he was now looking at me over his phone. He wasn't smiling with his mouth, but I could see it in his eyes.

"I can't wait until tomorrow," he said. With Kayci on one hip, he leaned over and gave me a sideways hug on his other side. I felt him kiss the top of my head, and I swear it still felt warm after his lips moved away.

"Me either."

My Dirty Past

Hope was crying in her room as I tried to make sense of my hair. I expected Jace to be there at any moment, and I was still in my bathrobe after a five-minute shower. It was all I could fit in since Miss Sunshine had decided to pull an all-nighter—this night, of all nights! Frustrated, I pulled my hair up into a messy bun and stormed into Hope's room.

"It's time for bed," I told her, trying to keep my voice sweet with clenched teeth. This only made her cry harder. She stood up against the crib railing and started to swing her leg over. "No, Hope," I said, moving over to her. As soon as I picked her up to put her back down, she threw her head back and howled. Her feet and arms went in every direction. "Not tonight," I groaned. I was furious with her, even though this wasn't her fault. All she knew was that she wasn't ready to go to bed, and I wasn't listening to her. "Fine," I growled, and picked her up and held her to my chest. Instantly, the tears were gone and she began to suck her thumb as she rested her head against me. "You're ridiculous, even if you're cute," I told her, and kissed her forehead. Charlie was in his study, and had agreed to take over Hope duty when I went out. But until then, she was on my watch. "You're just going to have to watch me get ready." I started to leave the room when I heard the doorbell ring. I paused, wondering if anyone was going to get it. No one else did.

"Well, here goes nothing," I whispered to Hope. I carried her to the door and peered through the peek hole. Jace. I took a deep breath, then let it out slowly before I opened the door. He grinned when I opened it, and then his grin widened when he saw what I was wearing.

"I totally approve. Let's go."

"Very funny," I said as I pulled my bathrobe tighter. I couldn't help noticing how good he looked in what *he* was wearing, and it was nothing but a button-up shirt and a pair of khakis. Nothing special, but he wore it well.

I moved aside so he could come in, and closed the door after him. "Hope's being a little difficult tonight and won't go to bed. I'm going to finish getting ready, if you don't mind waiting here for a bit."

"I don't mind," he said. "Do you want me to take her?"

I hesitated. *Do I?*

"I don't know. I'm not sure if she'll go with you. Besides, I don't want to bother you. It's no big deal for her to play in my room."

"It's no big deal for me to sit with her, either. Maybe I can even get her to sleep."

"I seriously doubt it." Still, I knew I'd get ready faster if she wasn't in my room, so I handed her over. Although she'd been crying only two minutes earlier, she went to him without an issue. "I'll be down the hall if she starts getting fussy."

"I can even text you," he said, holding up his phone with his free hand. Hope was snuggled against his chest as if she belonged there, and I had to turn and walk away before I started swooning too much. But I paused at the edge of the hall, watching as he found one of her books and settled onto the couch.

Don't go losing your head over some boy, Maddie.

I got ready as fast as I could, which meant it still took twenty more minutes. I curled my hair, but decided it looked like I was trying too hard, so I brushed it out and put it in a ponytail. There was a slight wave at the end; my curling efforts weren't completely wasted. I put on a dress and looked in the mirror. Too dressy—especially since we'd decided to go out for pizza the night before over text. I paired the dress with jeans, but it looked stupid. I took the jeans off and put on a pair of short, chunky boots. Now it looked sweet with a tomboyish edge. I could handle that. I did my makeup, and hated every color I applied to my face. I scrubbed it off and started over, this time just putting on clear lip gloss and a few coats of mascara. *Better.* I lined my eyes lightly with black, and the look was complete. I went through my earrings, trying on several pairs before deciding not to wear any. I wavered against taking a jacket or not. It was summer, but Petaluma evenings were often chilly. I settled on carrying a jean jacket.

When I reached the living room, I paused. Jace held his fingers to his lips. Hope was passed out against him, her head turned to the side as he continued to hold the picture book they'd been reading in front of them.

"I can't believe it," I whispered.

"Believe it," he whispered back. He set the book on the couch, and moved to get up. I started to grab her, but he shook his head, followed me to her room, and set her in the crib. She only moved slightly before curling up to sleep. We tiptoed out and I closed the door.

"How did you do that?"

"I have a few tricks I've learned over the years," he said with a wink. Of course he did. He had Kayci. Still, I knew how finicky Hope could be when it came to "her people." She wouldn't let just anyone hold her, let alone help her fall asleep.

"Let me tell Charlie I'm going." I went to Charlie's study and knocked lightly.

"Come in."

I opened the door and saw him bent over paperwork. He looked up, and I could see the tiredness in his eyes.

"Are you sure you're up for watching Hope tonight?" I asked. "You look beat."

"Is she still up?"

"No, but if she wakes up…"

"Maddie, she'll be fine. So will I. It's about time you went out and had a good time. Speaking of which, is that boy here? Do I get to meet him?"

I shook my head.

"Not yet," I whispered, hoping Jace couldn't hear us.

"I do hope I get to meet him soon," he said. I knew what he was hinting at. I hoped he'd get to meet him soon, too.

Jace drove us to Old Chicago Pizza. According to him, it was one of the best places in town to grab a slice. He parked on the main street, and we walked up the road, looking in shop windows on the way. It was nice to not be in a hurry, to not have to drag a toddler or two with us, to just hang out. I'd forgotten what this felt like.

We reached a brick building, and he followed me up the narrow stairs to the restaurant. The place was packed when we reached the top, conversations bouncing off the brick walls and every table taken. Jace gave the waitress our name, and we sat off to the side while we waited. Knowing it would be a long wait, he pulled out his phone and we played this game called, "Heads Up." He had me go first, telling me to hold the phone to my forehead while he gave me clues to the word displayed on the screen. He'd picked the "Accents & Impersonations" category, and immediately broke into some kind of cowboy accent.

"Uh, cowboy?" I said. He shook his head.

"No, think state," he said with a southern drawl.

"Texas?"

"Yes!" He told me to flip the phone up, and a new clue came out.

"Uh, we like cheese, doncha know," he said.

"Wisconsin," I said.

"I don't even know how you got that," he said.

"I don't either." I flipped the phone up. "That was awful."

"Bond, James Bond," Jace said in a Scottish accent.

"Oh shoot! I know this one!" I strained to remember. I could almost see his face, but just couldn't place him. "It's not Pierce Brosnan, is it?"

"Ay, that would not be correct," he said.

"Wait, you're Canadian now?"

"That's not a Canadian accent."

"Yes it is, it's—"

"You're wasting time," he said, "and I'm getting ready to go watch Indiana Jones, the best one. You know, the one where I played Indy's dad."

"Sean Connery!" I said as the bell dinged. "I get that one. I guess it." He reluctantly agreed, taking the phone from me.

"Fine, since you only got two," he said, and I smacked him on the arm.

After another twenty minutes, the game got old and the place was still packed. I was starting to feel hungry, and could practically taste the pizza. We sat in silence next to each other, willing the waitress to call our name by staring at her. She ignored us in response.

"You know this used to be a brothel, right?" Jace said.

"What? No, it wasn't," I said. "You're kidding, right?"

"It's true," he insisted. "This used to be the parlor to one of Petaluma's infamous bordellos. Ladies would entice customers from the windows." He gestured at a wall near us. "Once the customer made his choice, the couple would retire to one of eight rooms down the hall. Back in those days, this building was connected to a hotel, and visiting men could access it in secret from the second floor."

"Here in Petaluma? That's so hard to believe!" This piece of information contradicted everything I'd learned about Petaluma. Farming made up much of its history, mainly because of the chicken ranches that made Petaluma the "Egg Capital of the World" in the 1920s. We even had an annual "Butter and Egg Days" parade, where little kids dressed up like chicks and the town celebrated its heritage. It was very quaint and small town, nothing like Jace's story.

"Oh, believe it. This town has a dirty past. We've had brothels, saloons, speakeasies, and a few other skeletons in our past."

"How do you know all this stuff?" I asked.

"Well, the brothel stuff is on that sign over there," he said, pointing beyond me. I turned and saw a framed poster I'd never noticed before.

"You cheated," I laughed.

"Not really," he said. "I probably wouldn't have known about it if I hadn't eaten here a few dozen times with my family. But this is also stuff everyone knows if they've lived here all their lives. It makes this boring town interesting."

"I don't think Petaluma is boring at all," I told him. "It's so different from where I came from."

"And where did you come from?"

I told him about Gallup, describing what a boring New Mexico town really looked like. "The place is surrounded by desert, the buildings are old but lack the character Petaluma buildings have, and there's nothing to do, ever. I think the most interesting things about Gallup are that it was used in old western movies, and Route 66 runs through it. Other than that, though…"

"That doesn't sound all that boring," he said. "But I guess I get why you left. What made you come all the way to Petaluma? Did your stepdad get a job here or something?"

"My stepdad?"

"Charlie," he said. "At least, assuming he's your stepdad. You call him by his first name."

"Oh! No, Charlie isn't my stepdad, he's…" I wasn't sure how to explain the role Charlie and Viola played in my life. Luckily, the waitress finally called our name and led us to our table. We put the conversation on hold as we looked over the menu. Jace suggested a double-crust pizza with sundried tomato pesto, sausage, and artichoke hearts. It was different from the regular pepperoni pizza I was used to, but I trusted him when he said I'd love it.

"So, what have you done since graduation?" I asked, turning the topic away from me. I didn't want to discuss the past just yet.

"Sleep," he said with a laugh. "Actually, I've been kind of busy. I work at Petaluma Market, and they've scheduled a lot of daytime shifts since I'm out of school. That's been good; it'll help me save for the massive college loans I'll have in a few years. And, as you know, I babysit Kayci on my free days so my mom and stepdad don't have to pay for daycare."

"Kayci's your half-sister?"

"My mom remarried about five years ago. Tom. I like him okay. I mean, he makes my mom happy, but he's different, you know? Before he came around, it was just my mom and me. Things were simpler, but it was hard on her, doing it all without much help from my dad. While we had our own way of doing things, we also didn't have a lot. When Tom came around, that changed. She didn't have to work as hard to make things happen. He was super involved, which was both good and bad. I liked that he seemed interested in my stuff, like going to my baseball games or taking us out to dinner. But he also took on being my parent, too, which I hated. I didn't need another dad."

"How did things get better?"

"They didn't, at first," he said. "Tom asked my mom to marry him, and I didn't speak to her for a week after she told me she'd said 'yes.' Then we moved into the same house, and I was around him all the time. He got stricter after the wedding, and the two of us fought a lot. And then my mom got pregnant."

He shook his head. "I didn't even know she could still get pregnant. I mean, she was only in her mid-40s, but it seemed ancient to me to be having a baby. So when she dropped the news, I…" He looked at me and wrinkled his nose. "I wasn't exactly nice to her. I told her how old she'd be when that kid graduated, and how she'd be paying for the kid's college when she was retiring. I threw all this stuff in her face, and we got into a huge fight. She told me she wasn't even trying to have a baby when she got pregnant, and I told her she was pretty dumb to not know how birth control worked. We screamed at each other, and I was ready to pack up and move to Hawaii to be with my dad."

He paused and smiled. "Then Kayci was born," he said. "I don't know how it happened, but the world just stopped. I held her, and I could see her little hands, her little feet, her little everything. She was so tiny, so helpless. And I was so in love with her. We all were. She's kind of the glue that keeps us all together. Suddenly, Tom wasn't so bad; we even started to get along. My mom and I forgot we'd been mad at each other—we became a family. Kayci was the best thing that could have ever happened to us."

"That's why you don't mind taking care of her all the time," I said. He nodded.

"It's different having a little sister when I'm so much older. If we were closer in age, our relationship would be so different. Sure, we'd have more in common. But now, I appreciate her so much more. I don't fight with her because I want to protect her. I love being around her because she makes everything seem brand new. I mean, even the sky looks different when I'm with her because she makes me take the time to see everything."

We continued talking, mostly rehashing the playdate from the day before and talking about the girls, until the pizza arrived. The waitress set the plate on a pedestal in the center of the table. We each took a slice, and I covered mine with parmesan. I blew on it for a minute, then took a bite. It was probably the best pizza I'd ever had.

"Oh, my God," I breathed.

"Right? I don't think I can eat any other pizza because of this place," he said. He took another bite, closing his eyes. I did the same, savoring the flavor of the cheese and sauce melting in my mouth. I couldn't believe I'd never been there before.

"I've told you pretty much my whole life story," Jace said, and I opened my eyes to find him looking at me expectantly. "Now it's your turn. Tell me about you, and don't leave anything out."

The pizza was suddenly hard to swallow. I felt my palms get sweaty. He'd lived in a house his entire life, and had at least one parent who cared about where he was or what he was up to. And Hope was proof I didn't know how to use birth control, just like his mom. My boyfriend ditched me, I'd been in jail, and I knew what it was like to look in a garbage can for food. He wasn't ready to hear my story, and I wasn't ready to tell it. But which parts did I leave out?

"I found out I was pregnant at sixteen," I said. "And my dad kicked me out of the house." I told Jace about leaving New Mexico with my boyfriend, Jordan, but skipped the part where his dad tried to rape me. It wasn't my fault, but it was something that made me feel ashamed. I told him about the long drive to California, skipping the part where it was funded by the money from a stolen wallet. I told him how we crashed at his friend's house in San Francisco before moving toward Petaluma, but left out the part where we stole money before we left. Then I summed up the worst two days of my life by saying Jordan left me—not mentioning how I tried to steal some woman's wallet, got arrested while watching Jordan drive out of the parking lot, and how my parents abandoned me again after bailing me out of jail. I also skipped the part about being homeless for months while I was pregnant. Instead, I just told him the Winstons hired me to work for them, explaining Charlie and Viola's roles in my life and how we became so close they asked me to move in. I didn't tell him I handed my daughter to a fireman, intending to give her up, and if it hadn't been for the Winstons' generosity, I wouldn't even be Hope's mother.

I felt guilty about telling him a filtered version of my story. He probably didn't realize things didn't add up. Because he'd lived a more stable life, he didn't know to ask how I made money when Jordan and I didn't have jobs, or where I lived when Jordan and my parents abandoned me here. He took these things for granted; he'd never had to think about them. In his life, an adult had always been in charge, handling these things behind the scenes. It was different for me. I'd learned everything can change in a second, and the only person you could truly count on was yourself—and sometimes even that wasn't true.

"Whoa," he said when I finished. "I had no idea. I mean, I knew you had a baby young, obviously. But that other stuff… I mean, your parents actually kicked you out? Have you talked to them since?"

"No," I said, glaring at the table. When I looked up, I was moved by the way he looked at me with such concern. I softened my tense shoulders with a shrug. "Sometimes I'm tempted to call," I admitted. "I think my mom would talk to me. But mostly, I'm angry with them, especially now that I have Hope. Knowing how much I love her, and how much I would do for her, I can't understand how my parents could turn their backs on me when I needed them most. I made a mistake, but I was still their child." I lowered my eyes because I didn't want to cry. I'd mostly managed to move on by pushing my parents and Jordan out of my head. But when someone felt sorry for me, the despair I'd experienced every day would overwhelm me again.

"How did you juggle school and raising a baby?"

I figured he was changing the subject on purpose, and I was grateful for it. "It wasn't easy. I had to miss what should have been my junior year when Hope was a baby. By the time I started school again, I was a year older than everyone else. I already felt awkward, and knowing I was supposed to be a grade ahead made me feel like a total outcast. It didn't help once people found out I had a baby." I looked away and cleared my throat, embarrassed to admit I sometimes felt shame about being a mom. Every time I longed to fit in, I realized it was like wishing Hope away. "Anyway, I went back to school when Hope was almost a year old, and our house manager, Fátima, took care of her while I was gone. That was probably the hardest part, and I had a tough time making friends because I was so upset about leaving Hope at home."

That wasn't all of it, though. I felt guilty. I'd almost given her up; I'd almost abandoned her, like my parents abandoned me. To leave her while I went to school felt selfish. My brain told me I needed to do this so I could eventually support the both of us. But my heart ached to be with her. Every time I walked out the door to go to school, I felt like I was deserting her all over again. It took months to get over it. I'd had a hard time looking anyone in the eye. I felt like everyone would see all my mistakes. Being an outcast as a teen mom was one thing. If anyone knew I'd almost given her up, I'd be an outcast for life.

"Where's Hope's father in all of this?" Jace asked. "Does he call or send money?"

"No," I said, and looked down at my half-eaten pizza. It had been three years since I'd seen Jordan, and I still felt tied up when I thought of him. "I haven't seen him since he took off. To be fair, he doesn't know how to find me. Even if he did, I don't think he'd be any help." I looked up at Jace. "I think Hope is better off this way. Our lives are simple now. My life with Jordan was not." I left it at that, hoping he wouldn't ask me to elaborate, to reveal the messy parts of my life. Luckily, he just nodded.

"I lived without my dad most of my life," he told me. "I think my mom came to the same conclusion you did. It wasn't that he was a bad man, and she was good about keeping any negative thoughts to herself. But I grew to know that he just wasn't dad material, too unreliable. I'd forget this when I wasn't around him, but it all came back when I visited. He lived in this shack near the ocean. It had an incredible view, but it was only one room. He spent the mornings getting high and then going out to surf. Then he'd wait tables in the evening. I guess you could say he was a functioning pothead. He knew what he needed to do to survive while still having fun. He was more of a buddy than a dad. Visiting him was like going on a messed-up vacation. On one hand, it's Kauai. Everything's beautiful, the food is incredible, and, well, the girls around there are hot. But on the other hand, his house was a wreck. It smelled like mildew and I was always chasing chickens out of the house. He was high most of the day, and gone at night. I was pretty much on my own. When his girlfriend moved in, I made that my excuse to stop visiting. There wasn't room for me. But mostly, I didn't want to go." He paused, picking at his pizza. "I thought he'd put up a fight when I told him I couldn't visit him as much anymore. But he only said, 'That's cool,' as if it was no big deal he wouldn't see his son."

Jace glanced at me, and then looked down again. "Sorry, that's not where I was trying to go with this. What I mean is, I was fine with just my mom. I was better off with her, like Hope is better off with you. I miss my dad, or at least, I miss the dad I wished he could have been. When Hope gets older, she might feel the same way. It might take a while for her to understand why it's just the two of you, but it sounds like you have some good reasons to raise her on your own. One day she'll understand and appreciate all the sacrifices you've made for her."

"Yeah," I said. I bit into my now-cold pizza, chewing it as I thought about our similar stories. "You, me, and Hope," I said after I'd cleared my mouth. "We're so alike. We have messed-up childhood stories, and dads who let us down."

"True," Jace said, "but I think it's up to us to change our feelings about where we came from. My dad is off doing his own thing, and isn't much of a dad at all. But when I accept that and let him be my friend, everything feels like it's supposed to. I have a good life here in Petaluma with my mom and Tom. I don't need him to be my dad. Taking that expectation off him just allows me to love him for who he is instead of thinking about how he's let me down. For you and Hope, it's a little different. She doesn't know any better right now, but one day, she will. That's why it's important for you to figure out what you're going to tell her when that day comes. Your parents failed you. Jordan failed you. What they did was really terrible. But what if things had been different? What if your parents kept you in their home? You'd still be a child under their roof, influenced by their beliefs as you raised Hope. And I don't know what your life was like with Jordan, but I'm willing to bet it's not as great as it is now. It seems like you and Hope have a stable life with the Winstons, and have a lot of people who love and accept you for who you are."

"You're right," I said. Most of me believed him. It's why I tried to push thoughts about my parents or Jordan out of my head. But sometimes when I had trouble sleeping, I couldn't help it—I felt overwhelmed with hurt over how they all let me down. The anger stewed inside me, and I knew I'd never forgive them. I agreed that moving forward was the best way to overcome that resentment, but moving forward felt a lot like letting them off the hook.

They didn't deserve my forgiveness, and I'd never forget how they betrayed me.

Falling in Like

After dinner, Jace and I walked through downtown. We stopped in a shop that was Christmas all year-round, and he insisted on buying me a fairy ornament he saw me eyeing. I told him he could see it on my tree this Christmas, and felt both excited and nervous to say it. I couldn't guarantee tomorrow, let alone six months from now.

We crossed the street, reaching a cobblestone road that reached the railing that overlooked the river, and watched as two kayakers floated lazily downstream with headlamps to guide their way. Jace told me about the basic classes he'd signed up for at the community college for the fall, but also how he hoped to go on to culinary school. He wanted to open his own café one day, a place where he'd serve mostly soup with fresh-baked bread, sandwiches, and other comfort foods.

"I'll call it 'Soup and Stuff.'"

I told him I'd be studying viticulture and business management, and I was getting a head start through Charlie's training in the vineyard. With a week of work under my belt, I was starting to see this wasn't so bad. I'd gotten quicker in the field, and I was more excited for the fall when we could pick the grapes and start the winemaking process, but when it came to the business, I felt like I was taking on more than I could handle. It was just the first week, but it was all overwhelming, and the business side just wasn't exciting. I still didn't know if it was what I wanted to do with my life, or if it was just convenient. I felt guilty to want anything different since Charlie was handing me a profitable career.

Jace took my hand as he led me across the bridge. He stopped in the middle, but didn't let go of my hand. As he leaned against the railing, he ran his fingers over mine. We watched night bugs tease the water below, causing ripples through the reflection of the city lights. Every now and then, a fish jumped up to catch one of the unsuspecting insects. Normally, looking at the lights on the water would be enough. Petaluma at night never got old; there were so many layers to the town's natural charm. Tonight, however, all I could focus on was Jace's hand. It was casual the way he weaved his fingers in and out of mine, as if he wasn't putting any thought into it. I could think of nothing else.

"If the wine business isn't your thing, then what is?" he asked.

"It's not that it isn't my thing," I said. "It's just hard to get excited about.

"So, what would you do if you could do anything?"

I thought about this for a while. His touch made my head swirl. I knew I'd think better if he wasn't touching me. I didn't want him to stop.

"My favorite class was this general art class I took my junior year." I fixated on his brown eyes, the way they crinkled in the corner, the small freckle in one of them, the way he was touching me. *Focus, Maddie.* "It was where I could be me. It didn't matter that I had a baby at home, or some other kid spent his lunch break getting high in the bathroom, or another was a social outcast in normal settings. In art class, we were there to be creative, and I found out I was good at it."

I missed picking up the paintbrush, or shaping a piece of clay into whatever it decided to be. I hadn't done anything creative since. But with a toddler running around, taking care of Viola, and now working with Charlie, there wasn't much time leftover.

"I'm taking watercolor this fall, along with my studies," I continued. "I'm excited to see what else I can learn."

He was facing me now, his hand at my waist. He was listening, but his fingers gave me chills as he traced the top of my hipbone. I couldn't read what he was thinking, if this tiny movement was driving him as crazy as it drove me. *Does he know what he's doing?*

"What's your favorite kind of art?" he asked. *He has no idea. None. I'm sure of it.*

"All of it, really. I love sculpting, and how I never know what I'm making until the clay tells me. I like pencil drawing, seeing how different pressure creates different texture on the page. I enjoy photography, finding new ways to see things through the lens of a camera. My favorite is probably painting. Facing a blank canvas, there's so much possibility before I start, and I can create anything with just a few strokes of color."

His hands made my head spin. *Maybe he does know what he's doing.* I touched his arm and ran my hand against his skin. In the dim light, I could see his mouth twitch just before he took a sharp breath in. *Two can play at this game.*

"So what's stopping you from getting an art degree instead?" How could he keep asking me questions at a time like this? All I could do was focus on his mouth, trying to see if it would give away what he was feeling.

"I'm not sure if I could make a living with an art degree. The wine thing is a sure deal, and it will give Hope and me a good life. If I became an artist, I'd probably send us back into poverty."

"Poverty?" he asked. I realized part of my secret past had slipped out.

I shook my head. "It's a long story," I said. "I want to give Hope everything she needs to be comfortable until she's out on her own, and I don't think art can do that."

My hand was now resting on his arm, and his was still making lazy movements across my hip. I moved a little closer, and he tightened his hand over my hipbone. I caught my breath.

"I think you can make anything happen if you're determined enough," he murmured. I couldn't take my eyes off his mouth while he spoke. "From what I know about you, you're definitely determined."

His skin smelled like citrus and soap, and I couldn't stop breathing it in. Everything about him was consuming me.

"Jace." His name fell from my mouth. I didn't need to say anything else. He placed his hands on my cheeks, and I breathed him in as he lowered his lips to mine. He started out softly, and I parted my lips to invite him in deeper. My head spun as he teased me. He drove me crazy through his exploration. Everything around us disappeared as we spoke to each other without words. No one had ever kissed me that way. His fingers clutched my hair as my persistence grew. I wanted it to last forever. But then he pulled away.

"We have to stop," he said, his breath jagged. I shook my head, and he laughed. "Maddie, I want nothing more than to take you home with me right now and continue this in private. But I'm falling in like with you."

"In 'like?'"

"In like," he repeated. "I like you, a lot. I like everything you've shared about yourself, and things I know I'll learn over time. I like the way I feel when I'm around you, and how I think about you when I'm not. I like the anticipation of seeing you. I like the way you look at me, and the way your eyes light up when you're around your daughter. I like how sweet you are, how innocent you can be. And yet, I also like how there's a world of knowledge inside you that

I know nothing about, but see it whenever I look in your eyes. You're different from anyone I've ever known, and yet you're so familiar to me. I'm falling in like with you, and I want to see it grow deeper. But if I don't stop kissing you, I might never see that happen."

I groaned, burying my head in his chest. My heart was ready to burst, and every inch of my skin was tingling. It had been so long since I'd been intimate with anyone, and yet, if he'd asked me to go home with him, I would have. In that, I was glad he stopped when he did. I didn't need to lose my head over the first guy since Jordan who'd shown me any interest.

I looked up at him, and he leaned forward and planted a small kiss on my lips.

"Well then, we're just going to have to spend a lot more time together," I told him.

"Lots and lots of time," he said, taking my hand and walking me the rest of the way across the bridge. Then he took me home. He drove one-handed, holding mine with the other, and we let the radio talk for us. I felt both energized and exhausted. When we got to the house, he opened my door and walked me to the porch. Did guys still do this? I remembered the few times Jordan had picked me up from my parents' house, honking from the driveway to get my attention. At the end of the night, he'd drive me home, and then speed away before I reached the door. Jace was so different. It seemed old-fashioned. I liked it.

At the door, he gave me a hug. I stayed in his arms, liking the way he pulled me close and held me. I felt safe. I felt cherished. It was just a hug. It was everything. It was as if his embrace helped the world make sense.

He brushed his lips against mine. Neither of us tried to go further. I was certain he was thinking the same thing I was—we might not be able to stop if we started again. Already, I found him intoxicating. He pulled away and I inhaled his citrus scent once again, trying to memorize the way he smelled. He smiled, and then shook his head.

"Is it dumb that I don't want to leave you?" he asked.

"It's not dumb at all. I feel the same way."

"How is this possible? I barely know you, but I feel like I've known you all my life."

I gave him a weak smile. I was afraid to say anything more. *I've never felt this way. This makes more sense than it should. I don't just like you, I like like you.* I couldn't say any of it.

He kissed me again, said goodnight, and walked down the stairs. I stayed in the doorway and waved until he drove away. Then I went inside and shut the door. I closed my eyes as I leaned against it and slid down until I was sitting on the floor, a goofy smile plastered on my face. *Jace.* Was I naïve in hoping this feeling would never end? I couldn't wait to see him again, know him better, and get to the point of finishing each other's sentences or referring to ourselves as "we" instead of "I" or "me." I didn't want to lose the feelings I had, the intensity, the newness and excitement. I wanted to always feel surprised by him, even when I knew every inch of his body. When we fell in love—not if, *when*—I wanted to also remain "in like."

"Maddie, dios mio, thank goodness" I opened my eyes and saw Fátima coming down the hall. The look on her face replaced my good feelings with fear.

"Hope? Is she okay?"

"Hope is asleep. But Señora Winston, she is sick." I stood and followed Fátima to Viola's bedroom. Charlie was with her, holding her hand while she thrashed on the bed. Her eyes were closed, but she was fighting something only she could see. My heart raced seeing her like this. For a moment, I felt helpless…afraid…small. But something grabbed hold of me, and clarity intervened.

"Have you called the doctor?" I asked. Fátima nodded.

"Si, Dr. Kenneth should be here soon. I call him thirty minutes ago," she told me. I leaned forward to try to calm Viola. My hand brushed her skin, and the heat scared me.

"She has a fever!"

"Yes," Charlie said, "and we can't get her to calm down enough to try and bring it down. I'm afraid she's going to hurt herself."

The doorbell rang, and I rushed to answer, relieved Hope was sleeping through all this. I led Dr. Kenneth to Viola's room. He took one look at her before grabbing a pouch from his bag. From that, he pulled a syringe.

"I'm going to need you to hold her still," he told Charlie.

"I'll do my best," Charlie said, but he looked unconvinced. He threw his body over her as she tried to fight him off. I stood by, feeling completely useless as I saw her grab at Charlie, trying to get him off her. I knew she didn't recognize Charlie as her husband, and she was probably thinking the worst.

"I'm sorry, sweetheart," Charlie told her. "I'm not trying to hurt you." I could hear the pain in his voice, and knew how much this pained him.

Dr. Kenneth moved quick, administering the shot in her thigh. She calmed in seconds. Charlie got up, and she looked at us with droopy eyes. Eventually they closed, and she began to breathe deeply.

"How long has she been like this?" Dr. Kenneth, taking out a thermometer.

"It started a few hours ago," Charlie said.

The doctor pressed a button on the thermometer. It beeped, and he placed it under her armpit. A minute went by before it beeped again. When he looked at it, he frowned. "103.7."

"Do we need to take her to the hospital?" I asked.

"Not necessarily. She'll probably feel more comfortable here. Do you have ice packs? Or even ice you can put in a bag and wrap in a towel?" Fátima and I nodded. "Good, get a few and place them on her body. I brought saline with me, just in case, to help rehydrate her." He turned to Charlie. "Once her temperature is down, you and I need to discuss options." Charlie lowered his eyes and nodded.

An hour later, Viola's temperature had dropped to a manageable low-grade fever. The doctor instructed us to keep an eye on her to make sure her temperature stayed level, keeping her forehead cool with a damp cloth. He'd given her an acetaminophen injection and told us to give her Tylenol every four to six hours, as needed.

Before he left, Dr. Kenneth and Charlie went into the office and closed the door. I was curious, but Charlie's face was blank when they came out a few minutes later. He led Dr. Kenneth to the front door, ignoring Fátima and me.

"Just think about it, okay?" Dr. Kenneth shook Charlie's hand. Charlie nodded, and said goodbye before closing the front door.

"I think that's enough excitement for one night," he said, looking at me and winking. But I saw his sadness. "I'll check on Viola one more time before going to bed. Let's all get some sleep." He turned to Fátima. "Thank you for coming on such short notice." She nodded her head.

"De nada. Anything for you and Señora Winston."

I hugged Charlie goodnight, holding him a little longer than usual. I felt like he needed it—or maybe I did. When I let go, he kissed the top of my head, like a father would do for a daughter. He then went back into Viola's room.

Hope was sleeping, unaware of the drama. Usually she'd wake up from a creak of the floor, even when I tiptoed into her room. Knowing this, I crept to her crib. Thankfully, she stayed asleep, her little fist next to her mouth, her lips pursing as she dreamed. I watched her body rise and fall, her arm tucked over a stuffed pig, her favorite toy of the week. Her curls lay partially over her face, and I gingerly brushed them aside. She was so perfect, so precious to me. I wondered if I'd still feel this way when she became a teenager. Would it always seem this unbelievable that someone so wonderful came from someone like me?

I quietly closed the door and went to my door. I took my phone from my pocket and moved to charge it, but saw a text message on the screen.

Jace: *Is it too soon to tell you I had a really great time tonight, and I can't wait to see you again?*

I held the phone to my chest. Despite Viola's health scare, I felt everything falling in place. Life was good. Life was beautiful. I started typing into my phone.

Me: *I think you're supposed to leave me hanging a few days. You shouldn't be so sweet, either.*

Jace: *What I meant to say was, tonight was eh.*

Me: *Just eh?*

Jace: *Yeah. If eh means amazing and I can't wipe this stupid grin off my face. Ugh, there I go again. Should we just pretend I never texted and I'll try to ignore you?*

Me: *It's too late.*

My heart pounded in my chest as I tapped the next words.

Me: *Is it too early to tell you that I already miss you?*

I hit send before I changed my mind, then stared at the phone, waiting for his response. I didn't have to wait long.

Jace: *I miss you, too.*

Even if I wanted to, I couldn't stop smiling. It was plastered on my face. I couldn't remember the last time I'd felt this way.

I could see three dots on the screen, indicating he was typing again. I waited to see what he wrote.

Jace: *Is it too early to see you again tomorrow?*

Me: *It's never too early. See you tomorrow.*

Knocked-up Teen

When I woke, my first thought was Jace, and getting to spend another day with him. Then the rest of yesterday came back. Viola was sick, and I was planning to go out and have fun? Charlie would have his hands full, and need Fátima or me to help—and here I was, selfishly making plans for another date, assuming they'd babysit. What was I thinking? I needed to cancel. I picked up my phone to text, but paused when I saw the message Jace sent while I was asleep.

Jace: *Good morning sunshine. Would you mind if we made it a double date today? I forgot my mom needs me to watch Kayci, and I know the girls would like to see each other again.*

Charlie needed help, but how much help would I be with a bored toddler? Would it be better if Hope and I disappeared for a while?

Me: *Let me make sure no one needs me. Stuff came up last night, but I think this plan might be perfect.*

I got dressed and went into Hope's room. She stirred when the light from the hallway hit her face.

"Good morning, sunshine," I said, tasting Jace's texted words in my mouth.

"I not sunshine." Hope frowned, moving to get up. "I Hope." She started to climb over the railing.

"Whoa there, bucko." I grabbed her before she climbed over. "I know you can get out by yourself, but you need to wait for me to get you."

"Why, Mama?"

"Because you might fall." I smoothed the hair from her face, and she wrinkled her nose.

"I won't fall," she argued. "I fly."

"Really? Are you a bird, then?"

"No, I Hope!"

I set her down and started to pick out her clothes. She didn't wait for me, and ran to the open door, escaping before I could catch her.

"Hope!" I called, scrambling to my feet to catch her. She squealed as she rounded the corner to the kitchen. I found her hiding behind Charlie's legs, giggling as she peeked around at me. One look at Charlie's expression, and I could tell he wasn't into child's play this morning.

"Sorry, Charlie," I said as I moved to pick her up. She darted out of my reach, unwilling to end the game. Charlie offered a tired smile, and leaned down to scoop Hope into his arms. She threw her head back, trying to get him to roughhouse.

"Calm down, Hope," he said, his voice stern but kind. She got the message immediately, and the playing stopped. "What are your plans for today?" he asked me.

"Well…" I hesitated. Stay, or go? My guilt grew with every passing second. "I, uh, I thought it might be a good idea to get Hope out of the house for a while. I mean, I don't know what Viola needs, and I want to stay and help, but I also know how bored Hope will be; she'll probably be in the way. What would you like me to do?"

Hope was now playing with the pens in his pocket, pulling them out and dropping them back in.

"Honestly, I don't see any reason you need to stick around," he said. "Viola's asleep, and Fátima will be here soon. I don't have any work for you today, either. You should go out, enjoy that new car, spread your wings for a while. Maybe see that boy you went out with last night."

"Funny you should mention that," I said. "He has a little sister about Hope's age, and we were talking about letting the girls play together today."

"Well, that sounds more fun than hanging around here. Now tell me, he knows you're Hope's mother?"

"Of course."

"And how old is he?"

"His name is Jace, and he's eighteen." I gauged his reaction, feeling a bit embarrassed to admit I was older than he was. "He's a little younger than me, but it doesn't seem to matter," I quickly added. "We graduated from the same class."

"Have you thought about the future with him? How things will be if they get serious? Can he handle being a stepdad? Will he be able to hold a job and help support a family? Does he have a career choice in mind?"

"Whoa. We've just started seeing each other. I'm not marrying the guy."

"I know, but these are the kind of things you need to consider, even from the beginning. It's not just you anymore—it's you and Hope. Anyone you date could be a potential father figure to your daughter. If you're bringing Hope around this guy, I'm sure you believe he has potential."

"Well, yeah," I said. "I mean, I guess. He ran into me when I was with Hope, so it kind of happened without me making a decision. Plus, Hope and his sister met and they like each other. Today was about hanging out for a while, but also letting the girls get in some playtime. It's all pretty innocent."

"Nothing is ever innocent," Charlie said. Hope leaned for me, and I took her from Charlie's arms.

"This is," I promised him. "Look, I really like this guy. And he likes me. All that stuff you mentioned, I've thought about it. We've even talked about some of it. But I don't know everything about him, and I don't want to scare him away before we have a chance to start something by asking him if he'll be a good father to Hope."

"I know," Charlie said. "Look, I'm not trying to get in your business. But you and Hope, you two *are* my business.

I care about what happens to you, and I want the best for you. I don't want to see the two of you hurt."

"It's bound to happen," I told him. He made a face.

"I know," he admitted. "I've lived long enough to know that life isn't full of perfect outcomes. All I'm saying is pay attention. Keep your eyes open, whether it's this boy, or some other person you fall for. You may not feel comfortable asking these questions in the beginning, but you can figure out the answer by seeing how he presents himself, how he treats people around him, and what's important to him. Follow your heart, but follow your mind and intuition, too. Does that make sense?"

"Perfect sense," I said, leaning forward and kissing Charlie on the cheek.

Once we'd had breakfast, I dressed Hope and we headed out. My phone gave me directions through my car's speakers—another new novelty about this car. I wasn't sure I'd ever get used to this. I hoped I never would.

I pulled into the parking lot of The Funky Monkey where Jace had told me to meet him. I'd never been here, but he said it was a wild pizza parlor for kids that had games and live characters. I had to take his word for it because the windows were an opaque black.

Jace walked up holding Kayci. "How's Viola?" he asked when I got out of the car. I'd mentioned what happened over text, and it meant a lot that he cared enough to ask.

"She's okay," I said, sharing how she still hadn't woken up, but her temperature seemed stable.

"And how are you holding up?"

"I'm good." But then I gave him a wry grin and shook my head. "I'm a little stressed out," I admitted. "I needed to get out of the house. I'm looking forward to a chance to relax with some pizza while the kids play." Hope tugged at her belt as I tried to get her out. "Hold your horses, babe." She paused.

"I don't have any horses, Mama." Then she was back to tugging. "Hurry!" she insisted.

"I'm not sure I've properly warned you," Jace said. He wrinkled his nose when our eyes met. A memory of the previous night on the bridge flashed through my mind, and I shivered as I remembered our kiss, his hands in my hair, my body against his…

"Warned me about what?" I asked, shaking off the thought. As long as we had two little shadows with us, there would be no kissing today.

"You'll see."

He opened the door, and the sound of kids screaming, machines pinging, and music blasting overwhelmed me.

"Oh, Lord," I muttered.

"What?!" he yelled.

"I said, oh…never mind," I shouted back. I followed him inside, marveling at how so much energy could fill one room. There was a giant bounce house in the corner—kids had to travel through an obstacle course to get to it. Once there, they took turns catapulting off the walls. A skee ball game was on one wall, and a basketball hoop on the other. Tired parents surrounded the pizza counter, children tugging at their sleeves, and about a dozen kids clutched tickets as they looked at dollar store prizes at another counter. A few mechanical rides were near the tables, and these seemed more suitable for a couple of toddlers. Once we got in (they made us get matching hand stamps and took photos of me with Hope and Jace with Kayci before we could enter), I tried to steer Hope toward the rides. She wanted nothing to do with them.

"There, Mama!" She pointed toward the toddler-killing bounce house.

"Honey, you're too little for that." That was a mistake. Hope scrunched up her face, closed her eyes, and prepared to wail.

"It's okay," Jace said. "Let her go. It will be fine." Immediately, Hope opened her eyes and beamed. She pushed against me as Jace set Kayci down.

"Seriously?" I asked. "Look at that thing! Those kids in there are huge."

"Maddie, they'll be fine, I promise."

I clung to Hope as she fought against me. Kayci was halfway to the line outside the bounce house before she stopped, looking to see if we were following. She came back and tugged at Jace's shirt.

"Make the girl come," she insisted. "Come on, girl."

"That's Hope, remember? And hold on, we're almost ready." He turned to me. I was trying to figure out how I could politely leave. It was hard to tell one sound from another: music, screaming, and games felt like one huge pounding in my head. Plus, the place smelled like unwashed socks and greasy pizza.

"I don't know about this," I told him. All the good feelings I'd had after our kiss on the bridge were starting to fade.

"How about you follow them to the bounce house and I'll get the pizza. That way you can make sure Hope is okay the whole time. How does that sound?"

Not ideal. There was no way I was letting her out of my sight in this crazy hellhole. But as she struggled, I knew my options were slim. I nodded and he leaned over to give me a kiss on my cheek. In spite of myself, I inhaled his citrus scent, even through the sock-pizza reek. My cheek still felt warm when he pulled away.

Once Hope was on the ground, she and Kayci booked it for the line. I followed, but let Kayci show Hope around. It was interesting to see the difference between them: Kayci was completely sure of herself and Hope was innocent in so many ways. She proved this by trying to jump the line. Before I could stop her, Kayci stepped in and grabbed her hand.

"No, girl. We have to wait here," she informed her. Hope didn't even question. She stood obediently next to her as the line inched forward.

I wasn't sure what to do with myself. I was relieved to see a few others who were close to Hope and Kayci's age, but it didn't relieve my fear that older kids barreling through the course would trample them. I wanted to stand in line with them, but knew there was no way I'd fit through the course; it was obviously made for those four feet and shorter. Plus, none of the other parents were waiting with their kids. I noticed a few anxious mothers near the side of the bounce house, however, and I took my place next to them so I could witness my daughter's demise.

"The pizza should be ready in twenty minutes," Jace said in my ear, sliding his hand around my waist and touching his lips to my ear. As much as I enjoyed it, I brushed him away.

"You're distracting me," I told him, watching as the girls entered the narrow doorway leading to the adventure course. Jace chuckled, but didn't argue. Instead, he took my hand and we waited for the girls to become visible again. I held my breath the whole time, knowing anything could happen while I wasn't there to save her. If anything bad happened to her, I was never going to forgive him.

"Relax," he said, squeezing my hand and nodding at the rocking bridge above the bounce house. I looked, and let out my breath as I saw Hope and Kayci crossing the bridge. I heard Hope's squeal over the other screams, and relaxed my shoulders as I saw how much fun she was having. Kayci stood close by, and I noticed a slightly older girl had adopted them as her charges. She kept looking back, beckoning them to follow. They disappeared again, but this time I breathed normally. I even smiled when I saw them reach the bounce house, and laughed as Hope's face exploded into an open-mouthed shriek of glee. She fell numerous times, but it didn't seem to faze her.

"So this is what you do for fun, huh?" I asked Jace while I kept my eyes on the girls. I might have let the girls into this deathtrap, but I wasn't about to lose sight of them.

"Hardly," he admitted, and I broke my rule for a second, shooting him a look before zeroing in on the girls again. He laughed at that, then continued. "I've only been here for birthday parties with Kayci, and it's pretty much hell here. But she seems to love it, so I thought it might be fun if we spent the afternoon here. Bad idea, huh?"

I shrugged. My dislike for this place hadn't changed, but seeing how much fun the girls were having, I had to admit it wasn't a terrible idea.

"At least they'll get tired enough for a nap. *Hopefully*, that is." I nudged him, and he wrapped an arm around my shoulder. We watched as the girls made the most of their time in the bounce house, staying until we heard Jace's name over the intercom, signaling that our pizza was ready.

"Think you'll be able to gather up the girls while I get the pizza?" he asked. I wasn't sure I could, but nodded. He disappeared, and I squeezed my way to the front of the mom squad.

"Hope, Kayci, pizza's here," I called, leaning over the barricade to get as close as I could. They ignored me, continuing to bounce. I tried to get their attention several more times, but couldn't get them to leave. Breakfast suddenly seemed very long ago, and my stomach complained about its need for too-greasy pizza. "Come on, Hope," I said weakly.

"Here, let me." Jace said as he joined me. "Kayci, if you don't come out now, you won't get ice cream after your pizza!"

"Come on!" Kayci grabbed Hope's hand. Hope followed blindly as they made their way off the bounce house. The next stop was the ball pit. I was sure they'd forget the food once surrounded by a million balls, but Kayci triumphantly led them through, holding Hope's hand the whole time. They finally emerged, and ran around the line to reach us.

"Can we go again, Jace?" Kayci asked.

"After you eat, you can go one more time," Jace said. He looked at me and added, "But only once, okay?"

Kayci nodded, and we went to the table where our cheese and sausage pizza was waiting. Jace set a slice in front of Kayci, and I did the same for Hope. I started to cut her pizza, but stopped when I saw Kayci pick up her slice and start eating. There were a lot of milestones happening today, I realized watching Hope follow Kayci's lead. A few sausages fell off and rolled under the table, but Hope managed to get most of it in her mouth.

Jace kept his promise, buying the girls cups of ice cream before they ran back to the bounce house. I tried not to think about all that food jostling around in Hope's stomach while she bounced, reminding myself that she wasn't some delicate flower. I kept one eye on the girls while I helped Jace clean up. We were back at our station once they reached the front of the line. I was able to relax enough to enjoy Jace standing close to me, arm around my waist, hand resting on my hip. It felt natural, as if we'd been doing this forever. I wondered if this was how it would feel when things got more serious. Would it be like having a family? Would he be okay with that? Since he was the one who introduced us to The Funky Monkey, I figured he had to be family-minded. Why else would you enter a place like this on purpose?

It took a little coaxing to get the girls to leave the bounce house, though it seemed easier than the last time. They looked tired, and I could see Hope wiping her eyes. We scooped them up, checked out at the front desk, and then opened the door, squinting at the sunshine. My ears were ringing, and it took a few seconds to get used to the silence.

"Hey, Jace!" I heard, and we turned.

"Oh, no," Jace muttered, shaking his head. I was about to ask what was going on, but stopped when I recognized a group of guys heading our way. Colton, the guy who called, led the pack, followed by Jesse and Lance, and others whose names I couldn't remember. "Wait here,"

Jace hissed, placing Kayci's hand in mine. The move took me by surprise, even more when he left us behind to meet the guys halfway. I felt stupid standing there, not sure if I should follow his command to wait, or just leave. My feet remained planted.

"Hey, Colton! Ready for the big leagues? When do you leave for Vanderbilt?" Jace clapped him on the shoulder. Colton looked in my direction and grinned

"I should ask you the same thing, but it looks like you've already hit the big leagues. What are you doing, playing house?" he asked.

I shrank as he continued to look at me. I glanced at Jace, and felt my face redden when I saw him grimace.

"Come on, dude, it's not like that," he mumbled, turning back to Colton. He said it softly enough that he probably thought I couldn't hear it…but I did.

"Well, at least you know she doesn't play hard to get, right?" Colton continued. The others laughed. I suddenly felt small. I couldn't believe I'd been so stupid. I didn't wait for Jace to reply, spinning on my heel, ignoring Jace even as I heard him calling my name. I still had Kayci's hand in mine as I marched to the car, and she ran to keep pace with me.

"Don't move," I ordered her once we were at the car. I said it in a harsher tone than I meant to, and her face showed her surprise. I brushed aside my guilt, letting her hand go and shifting Hope in my arms so I could search my purse for my keys. I heard the guys calling after Jace, signaling that he was heading in my direction. Good. He could take his little sister and leave my life forever.

"Maddie, please," he said once he was at my side. I found my keys and pulled them out, then dropped them.

"Shit," I said, and then huffed when I realized there were young ears listening to me swear. Jace picked up my keys and held them out. I grabbed them and unlocked the door. "Just go, Jace. We're through."

"Let me explain," he pleaded.

"Explain?" I buckled Hope into her seat, but I was being too rough in my hurry. She started to whimper.

"I don't wanna go," she sniffled.

"Too bad," I snapped. Wrong move. Hope burst into tears. In response, Kayci started crying, too. Now we had two crying toddlers, I was pissed, and Jace was still trying to make me his good time. I grabbed two emergency packages of goldfish crackers from my purse, opened them and handed one to each girl. The bait worked; they quieted down. "Look, this isn't happening," I said, turning to Jace. "In fact, it's never happening. If you're looking for an easy lay, I'm not your girl. You really think I'm going to give in to you just because I have a kid?"

"No! I don't!" Jace said. It was his turn to look angry. I didn't care. I wanted everyone to feel as angry as I did. "I should have punched Colton for what he said about you. He's a dick, and he's always been a dick."

"But you're friends with him," I retorted. I wasn't ready to believe him, but the fire in his eyes was wearing me down.

"We used to be friends. But then he became some big baseball star, and his ego took over. He became someone I couldn't stand, along with all his buddies."

"And you're one of them."

"It's complicated," he insisted. I put my hands on my hips, waiting for his explanation. "Thing is, when you're in, you're in. To leave is social suicide. I had no choice but to hang out with the guy. No one leaves Colton's group by choice. If I left, I'd become an outcast."

"So that's what you're worried about? If you stand up to him, you become an outcast?"

"No! I'm not worried anymore. We're out of high school, and I don't have to play the game."

"Then why didn't you tell him off? Why didn't you defend me when he basically called me a whore?" I hoped with all my heart Kayci and Hope weren't listening too hard.

"Because he had me outnumbered seven to one," Jace said. "I didn't stand a chance. And…" he paused, giving me a weak glance. "And I guess old habits die hard." He shook his head. "Maddie, I'm sorry. I should have told him off. I should have said so much more than I did. I shouldn't have just let him throw out a comment like that without teaching him a lesson. But the guy intimidates me. I froze up when I saw them. I knew they were going to say something I'd regret you hearing, and I was trying to keep him away from you."

"Is it true, though? Are you with me because you know I've done it before?"

Jace looked at me without speaking. Then he looked down at Kayci.

"Hey girl, want to hang out in the car with Hope for a second?" She nodded, and I moved aside so he could put her in the back seat next to Hope. He closed the door behind her, and then he closed the space between us. With his finger, he tilted my chin up so I was looking at him. I aimed to keep my heart hard, holding on to my pride as he looked into my eyes.

"I care about you," he said, "but I'd be lying if I said I didn't want to know what it's like to be as close to you as humanly possible. But we're not there yet, and I don't plan to be there for a long time. I want to get to know you first. When it comes time for us to be intimate, I want to make love to you, not just have sex. But I'm not making love to you until I'm *in* love with you, and when I know you love me back." He leaned closer to me as he was talking so by the time he was finished, his mouth was only an inch or two from mine. He lingered there, and I knew he was waiting for my permission. I didn't move, wondering if I could actually trust him. What if he was just saying the right things so I wouldn't push him away? What if the joke was on me, or would be if I chose to believe him? What if I was being a fool for believing he was telling the truth?

But what if I walked away and lost someone I could fall in love with? What if trusting him ended up being the best thing I could do for Hope and myself?

I leaned toward him and pressed my lips to his. I felt his breath escape against my mouth, and his arms around my shoulders. He kept his kiss gentle, his lips soft and tender as he continued to seek my approval.

I followed him in my car to his house, and we put the girls down for a nap. As we'd hoped, they fell asleep easily, allowing us time to be quiet together. I felt raw with so many feelings and doubts. I didn't want to talk about them; I wanted to be held by someone who cared about me. I wanted that person to be Jace.

He turned on a movie, and I only half-watched it as the questions kept stabbing. *What if he's too young to be involved with someone like me? What happens the next time we run into his "friends?" Can he handle this? Can I?* My mind replayed the questions Charlie asked me that morning, the leers and comments Colton and his friends threw my way, the promises Jace gave me. Was I being fair to him by sticking around?

"What are you thinking?" he whispered, resting his lips on my forehead. I closed my eyes, forcing my doubts to the side. I snuggled closer, and felt his arm tighten.

"How good this feels," I said, pressing my cheek against his chest, breathing in his citrus scent. I deserved this. He deserved this. We could make this work, as long as I stopped trying to over-explain everything to myself. Jace was exactly the right person for me, and I was not about to lose him.

"I can't wait to fall in love with you, Maddie," Jace murmured into my hair.

Future Tripping

"Bird."

I looked up from the book I was reading in Viola's room. Her eyes were closed, her brow furrowed. It had been two days since her condition had gotten worse, and we were all worried. She still had a fever, though it never spiked as high as the first night. Fátima and I took shifts so she was never alone. Mine were generally during Hope's naptime and after she went to bed.

While Viola had been sick before, this was different. Charlie came in as often as he could, even just to hold her hand. When he did, I left the room so they could be alone, in case those were the last moments he'd have with her. The past two nights he'd stayed late, nodding off in the chair next to her bed. Tonight I saw the tiredness across his face, and I insisted he get some sleep, promising I'd call for him if her fever spiked again.

I looked at the clock next to her bed. 10 p.m. I'd been sitting in a rocking chair for three hours, and my bones were starting to ache. I set the book down and got up to stretch. Then I walked over to Viola and removed the cool cloth. Her forehead was still warm, but nothing alarming. I checked the pad she was lying on, and wasn't surprised to find it wet. Waking her to go to the bathroom or eat had been an ordeal over the past few days.

Earlier this evening, Charlie admitted the doctor talked to him about putting Viola in hospice care. That's all he told me, but it was enough. I could tell he wasn't comfortable with the idea. It would mean accepting she was dying, and I knew Charlie wasn't there yet.

I wasn't there yet.

I watched her sleeping, her face at peace as she breathed in and out. Her hair was in a braid to keep it from tangling, and I moved it so that it lay straight down the left side of her chest.

I thought back to the day after Hope was born. I'd woken up that morning in a clean bed, wearing one of Viola's old nightgowns, and covered in shame as I realized what I'd done—I'd given up my daughter. When I joined the Winstons in the kitchen, they were waiting for me. They fed me, they reassured me, and then they gave me back the chance to be Hope's mother.

When we went to the hospital, Charlie handled everything. All I had to do was be there to answer questions. I felt ashamed at what I'd done, and would have felt alone had Viola not been there holding my hand. She never left my side. A social worker met with me, and though she was kind, I felt overwhelmed as the questions continued. Every time I grew tense, Viola squeezed my hand tight. Charlie protected me from dealing with more than I could handle, but Viola made sure I didn't lose myself in the process, and kept me anchored until Hope was back in my arms.

Now as she slept, I brushed my hand over her cheek. She'd been the mother I never had, nurturing me as if I were her own. If she were able to talk with me, I knew she'd reassure me that everything was going to be okay. She'd tell me not to be scared, because *she* wasn't scared. She'd comfort me and do whatever it took to take my fear away, even though she was the one dying. She'd love me, and tell me until she took her last breath.

"I love you," I whispered, stroking her downy skin. "Let's get you cleaned up." She kept her eyes closed, but I saw them moving behind her lids as I removed the soiled covers and hospital gown. I replaced the wet pad with a clean one, and then washed her skin with a sponge and warm water. She frowned as I did so, but still kept her eyes closed. Once she was clean and dry, I put a fresh gown on her, covered her back up, and kissed her forehead. It was cooler than before. She moved her lips a few seconds before speaking.

"Bird."

I wished I knew what it meant.

She began breathing deeply again, and I knew she'd fallen asleep. I tiptoed out the door and went to the kitchen for a snack.

"How is she?" Charlie asked. I jumped, not expecting him to be there. I thought he'd been in bed for hours.

"You scared me!" He shot me an apologetic smile. "She's good. No fever at the moment, but she did wet the bed. I changed her and she's sleeping again. Which is what you should be doing." I took the cereal from the top of the refrigerator and poured us each a bowl. I added milk and a spoon, and pushed his bowl toward him. "What are you doing up? Can't sleep?"

He took a bite, nodding as he chewed. "Thanks," he said, tilting his head toward the cereal. "And no. I guess I have too much on my mind." He inhaled sharply, his mouth set in a line. "I think I need to seriously consider hospice." I nodded in agreement.

"It can't hurt," I said. I wasn't quite sure how to respond, how I'd feel in his shoes. I knew how hard this was on me, I could only imagine what he was going through. "If this ends up being nothing, we just stop the hospice care. But right now…" I took a deep breath, searching for the right words. Finally, I just chose brutal truth. "I don't think I can handle it if she dies while on my watch," I admitted. "I mean, Fátima would probably know what to do, but I won't. Plus, it will help Viola so much more if this truly is the end."

"I know," he said. He stirred his cereal, and I knew the rest would go down the drain.

"You should get some rest," I said.

"I know," he said again. And then he did something I didn't expect. He put his face in his hands and started to shake. I got up and wrapped my arms around him, holding him while he cried. At first he kept his face hidden, trying his best to remain silent as he sobbed. But soon, his arms were around me and he was crying openly. I couldn't help crying with him, but my tears were for him. I ached over what he was going through. None of us were ready to say goodbye, but this would be hardest on him.

"It's going to be okay," I told him, because that's what you're supposed to say in a moment like that. I knew it was true, but I didn't know *how* it would be true. One day at a time, I guessed. How did you let go of someone you'd loved for decades? How did you prepare for that moment when they were no longer in your life?

He let go of me and wiped his eyes. "Sorry," he murmured, and I saw he was embarrassed. Since I'd known him, he'd been the strong one. I'd rarely seen him cry. But he'd seen me cry many times—from sleepless nights with Hope to sheer frustration when she wouldn't listen. Now, he needed me to be the strong one.

I took his hand and looked him in the eyes.

"Don't ever apologize for your tears," I told him. "Your feelings are real, and what you're facing with Viola is both scary and heartbreaking. You've loved her for most of your life. You deserve every moment you need to release some of that pain you're feeling. I'm telling you the same thing you would tell me if I were crying in front of you—it's okay to cry."

He sighed and squeezed my hand. His eyes were still watery, but the tears stopped.

"I love you," he said.

"I love you, too." He leaned forward and gave me a kiss on the forehead. Then he picked up his bowl of cereal, dumped the soggy remnants, and placed the dish in the dishwasher. With a nod, he left the room to go to bed.

I popped a piece of bread in the toaster and checked my phone for any messages. There was a text from Jace, and I felt guilty to see it had come three hours earlier. I hadn't seen him since the weird date at The Funky Monkey. Even though we'd ended it on a good note, I still felt uneasy. The more time I spent away from him, the more troubled I felt. We'd tried to hang out, but with Viola as sick as she was, I was needed here—even with a toddler in tow. I missed him, and I knew being near him would help calm my fears, but there was too much going on around the house.

Me: *Hey. Sorry. Busy night.*

Deep down, I knew I was scared. I kept thinking about everything I had to lose if I gave him my heart. I could get hurt. I could forget how to be independent. I could fall in love only to find out he didn't love me the same way. I could allow Hope to believe he'd be in our lives forever, only to have to pick up the pieces if he decided this kind of life was too much for a teenager.

Jace: *It's okay. How you holding up?*

What am I thinking? How can I have a relationship at all right now? If I weren't already a mom, *I* wouldn't choose this life. It's not that I wouldn't choose Hope; I would in a heartbeat. But I wouldn't choose giving up the last years of my childhood to deal with colic, breastfeeding, dirty diapers, potty training, temper tantrums, stretch marks, lack of sleep...

Me: *I'm good. Viola seems to be getting better. But the doctor has suggested we put her on hospice.*

Could I ask Jace to take on any of this with me? I knew he was familiar with little kids because of his sister. But it was different than raising a child. He could always hand Kayci over if she got difficult. He didn't have to stay up all night if she got sick. He didn't have to worry about which preschool she'd get into, how to raise her so she'd grow into a decent adult, even how to pay for her college. Could I really ask him to take on that kind of life with me?

Jace: *I'm so sorry. I bet this is hard for all of you. Is it too late to call you?*

I looked at the clock; it was just after midnight. Knowing Hope, she'd be awake at six. I'd be hurting later, for sure. But I wasn't tired yet.

Me: *I can talk for a few minutes.*

My phone rang a few seconds later.

"Hey. You okay?" he asked. I closed my eyes at his voice. Hearing him, his voice subdued some of my worry.

"I'm okay," I told him. "I've known this was coming for a while. It's just hard to accept that it might actually be here. I'm more worried about Charlie, though. He's not taking it well."

I briefed him on how the evening went, including Charlie's tears.

"He's just not the same anymore, and I'm not sure he ever will be."

He sighed, and it sent a warm wave through me. I shook my head. *Stop being so affected by him.*

"This has got to be hard on him," Jace said. "No one wants to live longer than the person they love the most." He paused, and we let the sound of our breathing fill the silence. "I want to see you tomorrow."

"Jace."

"Hear me out. I know things are rough right now. I know your family needs you. But I need you, too."

"You hardly know me," I pointed out.

"We already had this conversation. I *want* to know you. I want to be around you. This is supposed to be exciting and fun, but I can feel you pushing me away."

"Viola's been sick."

"I know. I feel selfish for saying anything. But I know you have moments when you're not taking care of Viola. You haven't even wanted to talk on the phone."

"I have a daughter. I have a life. I have so many things going on beyond helping Viola get better. I'm sorry I don't have the time or energy for a social life right now. But this is what my life is like."

I stopped, even though I had more to say. I wanted to tell him he wasn't ready to be with a single mother. I knew it was true. But I also didn't want him to believe it. As much as I knew I needed to keep distance between us, I wasn't ready to let him go.

"Let me come over tomorrow," he said.

"Are you even listening to me?"

"I've heard everything you've said. That doesn't stop me from wanting to see you. I won't get in the way. I can help with whatever needs to be done. Put me to work. I'll fold laundry, take care of Hope, even help you take care of Viola. I just want to be around you. Please say yes."

The best thing I could do was say no. Everything in my head was telling me to say no. I knew I should break things off, because if it wasn't taking care of Viola, it would be something else getting in the way of me living a normal life or worthy of dating a normal guy.

"Yes," I said, even as I shook my head no. *What is wrong with me?*

"Thank you." I could almost hear his smile through the phone. I couldn't help smiling, too.

He got there at 9 a.m. Knowing he'd be early, I'd managed to get a shower in and put on a little makeup. I had pancakes cooking, and Hope was in her booster seat, humming as she played with her food.

"Wow, that smells delicious," he said, leaning in for a kiss. I turned my head and offered my cheek, as if Charlie or Fátima could see us, as if they'd actually care if a boy like Jace kissed me in the kitchen. When he pulled away, I ignored the amused look on his face, as well as his raised eyebrow.

"Pancakes?" I asked.

"I'd love some."

The air around us was different than it was the last time we'd seen each other, at least at the end of the date. It felt awkward. My mind was racing with thoughts of his kiss, mingled with questions that had troubled me over the past few days. We ate breakfast in near silence. Occasionally, one of us would comment on the food, or something Hope was doing. It was clear we both felt unsure about how to act.

"Up, Mama!" Hope said, pushing her food onto the floor and trying to shove the table away. She knew it wouldn't move, and I found it both ridiculous and amusing that she tried, anyway.

"Patience, little girl," I said. I started to clean her mess, but Jace brushed me aside.

"I've got it." He bent down and began collecting the torn-up pancakes on the floor.

"Thanks," I said, lifting Hope. I wiped her hands and face, and set her down. She immediately went to Jace.

"Where's KK?" she asked, leaning against him. Her familiarity with him both moved and troubled me. What if this thing between Jace and me didn't work out? There was the possibility he'd be out of our lives as fast as he'd come into them, and I'd allowed her to get to know him and be familiar with him. I was failing at dating as a single parent.

"Sorry. KK's home today. But I'll bring her tomorrow, all right?" My inner alarm went off as he made plans with my daughter that he hadn't discussed with me. He must have sensed my frustration, because he looked up at me. "Is it okay if I come back tomorrow?" I nodded yes, unsure what else I was supposed to do. I felt confused. I actually wanted to see him more. I loved how it felt to be with him the night we went out to dinner, and how we ended our last date. But now, all I could do was keep building up the wall he kept trying to tear down.

Fátima came out of Viola's room and closed the door. She gave Jace a warm smile. To me, she raised her eyebrow.

"This is my friend, Jace." I ignored her silent message. "Jace, this is Fátima. She basically runs our whole house, and helps take care of Viola and Hope."

"It's nice to meet you." Jace extended his hand.

"Con mucho gusto," she replied, but her tone suggested she was aware of the unspoken relationship between us. I gave her a look. "I go back to work now," she said, hiding her grin behind her hand.

"How's Viola?" She turned serious, removing her hand and giving a slight nod.

"Muy bueno. Her fever is gone, but she's very sleepy. Señor Winston is meeting with hospice today."

"I'm glad he's doing it."

"Same," she agreed. "Are you helping Señor Winston in vineyard today?"

I shook my head. "No, he told me to take the week off. He said my focus should be on Viola this week, since he's too busy with the business and paperwork to train me."

"Don't worry about Viola," she told me. "She's fine today, and I'll take care of her. Go out. The sun is shining. It will be good for Hope." She gave me a pointed look. I looked back at Jace. Hope was busy flirting with him. I looked back at Fátima.

"Don't start," I whispered.

"He very cute," she whispered back.

"I know," I moaned. "I'll talk to you later." She nodded, then left out of the kitchen.

"Whispering about me?" Jace asked, looking up at me from where he was sitting.

"Eavesdropping?" I laughed.

He motioned for me to come over. I sat next to him, and he took my hand.

"Stop worrying so much," he told me. I leaned my head against his shoulder, focusing on how comfortable it was to be next to him. It felt so much better than keeping my guard up.

We took Hope out to the backyard and let her dig in the dirt while Jace helped me with the garden. He was surprisingly good, even though he said he'd never done it before—his mom was the gardener, not him. But he knew the difference between small plant shoots and weeds, and helped me clear the beds in no time. It was starting to look like Viola's garden again. I hung a few hummingbird feeders near the deck, and Hope laughed every time a small bird swooped in for a meal. Earlier this week, I'd unearthed a few stone angels from underneath the weeds, and Jace wiped the grime from their surfaces to reveal pale stone features. The garden still looked like a jungle, but I kind of liked it that way. The wisteria covered the fence on one side of the garden, and tall flowers guarded the leafy overlay. Jace tied off a few towering foxgloves to keep the stems from breaking, and even figured out how to get more shade in the garden by stapling netting over the trellis. We had half of it covered in just a few hours. He told me he'd bring more netting the next day when he'd come over. I stopped cringing when he referred to the future, instead wanting to believe in tomorrow, and the next day, and every day after that. By lunchtime, we'd completed a ton in the garden.

"Hungry?" I asked Jace. Despite the pancakes at breakfast, my stomach felt ready to rumble.

"I hungry, Mama!" Hope said, abandoning her dirt pile. She lifted her dirty hands toward me, and I scrunched my nose as I picked her up.

"How about a bath, and then lunch?"

"No, Mama. Hungry!" she cried.

"I know, baby. But you're too dirty to eat. We'll make it quick."

She whimpered, but I ignored her as Jace and I went into the house. I led him to my bedroom. He sat on the bed while I turned on the water for Hope and stripped off her dirty clothes.

"So, this is your room, huh?" he asked. I glanced over in time to see his sly smile.

"Don't get any ideas, mister," I said with a laugh. "This is probably the most intimate moment you'll have with me here in the Winstons' house."

"I figured," he said, also laughing. "My house is kind of the same. It looks like we have a little bit of a problem."

"Let's not get ahead of ourselves here."

"I'm just planning for the future," he said with a wink. "The-super-far-away-but-still-often-thought-about future." I rolled my eyes at him, and put Hope in with the foaming bubbles. She played with the foam as I scrubbed. By time I was done, the water was dingy and she was wiping soap in her eyes. Thank goodness for tear-free suds. I cleaned the bubbles from her face, let the water out, and wrapped her in a towel.

Jace poked at her, making her laugh while I dried her and slipped a shirt over her head. When she was dressed, he picked her up and airplaned her to the kitchen. In spite of my reservations, I liked how comfortable he was with her. It offered a look at what it could be like in the future.

Hope barely ate any of her sandwich; the sun and bath had tired her out. I didn't force it, but rescued her sandwich before she could throw it on the floor. I wrapped it for later, and then lifted her from her booster seat. She didn't fight when I put her in the crib. Instead, she pulled up her blanket and closed her eyes as I left.

"Think we can go for a walk while she's napping?" Jace asked. I cringed. He didn't understand I couldn't just leave her, assuming someone else would watch her. I wanted to tell him this. Instead, I let the irritation stew as I nodded.

"Let me check if Fátima can watch her while we're gone."

Fátima was in the laundry room, pulling the dry clothes out of the dryer. "Would you be able to listen for Hope while we go for a short walk?" I asked.

"Sorry, mija. After I fold these, I promised Señor Winston I would pick up Señora's medicine. Maybe he is able to?"

I winced, not wanting to bother him. I nodded, and went to find him, anyway.

"Charlie?" I tapped on his office door.

"Come in," he said. As he usual, he was at his desk, a serious expression on his face.

"Jace and I would like to go for a walk while Hope takes her nap. We'll be back long before she wakes up. Can you listen for her in case she wakes up early?"

"Yes, yes. That's fine," he said, never looking up. I paused, wondering if he'd heard me. But then I decided I was worrying too much.

"Thanks," I said, and left him to his paperwork.

"Ready?" I asked Jace.

We left the house and walked along a path that bordered the Winstons' property, leading into the hills behind the house. We passed a large barn, one I always peeked inside whenever I passed by. Not this time. It felt like we were on a mission, and things felt too strange. I kept pace in front of him, leading the way through a canopy of trees, and then across the clearing on the other side. If I looked to my left, I would have seen a view of my whole neighborhood, and the hills that surrounded it. I'd be able to see my house, and the acres of vineyard. I could call out, and Charlie would probably hear me. If he called back, I might even hear him.

But this wasn't the time and place. Neither Jace nor I said a word, and I kept my gaze on the path ahead of me. I felt my walls building up again, and when he reached for my hand, I automatically tensed up.

"Maddie, stop," he said, holding my hand tightly. I had no choice but to stop with him. I looked at my feet, unsure of what to say.

"Jace, I—"

"Don't say anything." He let go of my hand. "Just trust me, okay?" I nodded, looking up into his face. "Close your eyes." I did. And then I waited.

And waited.

And waited.

I listened for his footsteps, his breathing, anything to give me a clue what he was doing. Instead, I heard the birds around us, the breeze rustling through the trees, the cicadas in the tall grass around us.

"Breathe, Maddie," he said in my ear. He wasn't touching me, but I could feel his chest near mine. I could smell his citrus scent mingling with the earthy smell of the trail. I could hear each breath he took. And then, I could taste him as he covered my mouth with his—capturing me, caressing me, claiming me. I couldn't fight him even if I'd wanted to. I met each of his kisses, raising my hands from my side to hold on to him and draw him closer. He pulled me in, teasing my tongue with his in a way that made me dizzy. *I can't. I can't. I can't.*

"I can't," I told him, pushing him back and catching my breath. My body felt betrayed by my defenses. Every inch of me was screaming, wanting me to give up my inhibitions and let him take me right there on the trail. But I just couldn't.

He groaned, clutching his head and turning away. My heart dropped at his reaction, and the fire in my belly began to cool. He turned back, and his expression softened as he lowered his hands.

"It's okay," he reassured me, coming over and wrapping his arms around me. "I just wasn't expecting your reaction." I nodded into his chest, then I gently pushed him away so the hug would end. He let go, and I saw the disappointment on his face.

"What's going on?" he asked.

"Nothing."

"Bullshit."

I looked at him sharply. "What?"

"I call bullshit. Something is going on, and you're not talking about it. Now I want to know what it is."

"It's—"

"Don't say 'nothing.' Have the decency not to lie to me. There's something. Is this about Colton and those guys? Because I swear to God, I'll go over to his house right this minute and show him exactly how I feel about the way he talked about my *girlfriend*."

I closed my eyes when he called me that, both enjoying it and wishing he'd never said the word. I shook my head.

"No, it's not that. We already talked about that. It's fine."

"Then, have you lost interest?"

"No."

"Okay, is there someone else?"

"No, Jace. It's not that."

"Then what is it? Because when we saw each other last, I thought we were good. But now, everything's changed. *You've* changed. And I don't understand how things can be so different in just two days."

"Give me a second!" I said. He stopped talking. "I just need a second to think, okay?" He nodded, and found a stump to sit on. I was too amped up to sit. Every part of me was jumping out of my skin. I paced, trying to make sense of what was going on inside me. I didn't know what

I wanted, what I didn't want, what my problem was. Why was I pushing him away?

"I'm scared, okay?" I told him. He didn't answer, but gave a slight nod. "I've never done this before. My last boyfriend was Hope's father, and he wasn't exactly the best choice I could have made. I didn't know it at the time, and even when he abandoned me, it took me a while to recognize how terrible he really was. And now, I've been single the past three years, raising Hope with the help of this new family of mine. All the people who were supposed to be there left me when I needed them most. I'm scared to let you in, because if I need you, you might leave me."

"No, Maddie, I—"

"Let me finish!" I yelled. He stopped talking, but I saw tears in his eyes. I looked away. I didn't want to see him cry because then I'd cry, too. "I know you think you won't leave me. And it's probably true. But it doesn't stop me from being scared, because besides the Winstons, people leaving me is all I've ever known." I took a deep breath. He sat on the stump, hands clenched. "I'm also afraid of what I'm asking of you by letting you into my life. It's not just me you're with, it's Hope and me. I signed on for this life, but you didn't. You're stepping into something you have no idea about."

"That's where you're wrong."

"Just because you have a little sister doesn't make you an expert on being a parent," I said. "It might make you familiar with what a kid that age is like, but at the end of the day, it's your mom who's responsible for her, not you. She's the one who has to worry when Kayci's sick, or how to afford daycare for her, or juggle doctor's appointments with a full-time job."

"That's true," Jace admitted. "But I know what's going on. I'm there when she worries about these things."

"Fine, but you have no idea what it's like to be a single mother."

"Maddie, I was raised by a single mother!" he shouted, standing up. I glared at him, though I didn't know why I was angry. I'd been yelling this whole time. But now that he'd raised his voice, I was ready to fight.

He took a deep breath and sat back down. "Can you stop pacing?" he asked. "It's making me nervous. Can you just sit with me here? Can we talk instead of shouting?"

I didn't say anything for a moment, and my hands stayed clenched. Finally, I nodded. I found a stump far enough away so he couldn't touch me.

"I know you're afraid," he said. "I saw my mom go through this time after time. When she first started dating Tom, she was a wreck. My opinion of him mattered way more to her than it should have. She almost called it off several times because I refused to warm up to him. Thank goodness she saw it through, because Kayci wouldn't be here. Plus, he's not such a bad guy. But I got to see firsthand how nerve-wracking it is to try dating while raising a kid. You're lucky Hope is little. She's young enough that she doesn't know to try to hate me first. I have that going for me, but I know that doesn't take away your hesitation to let your guard down and allow me to fall in love with you."

I couldn't look at him when he said it. I thought of that moment in the parking lot when he said he wanted to fall in love with me, but here I was trying to break up with him.

"I want the chance to fall in love with you. Even more, I want you to fall in love with me. I know that's a lot to ask of you right now, and I'm not expecting your feelings to change overnight, but I think there's something here that's really worth it, and I want to go there with you" He was looking at me with such intensity I had to look away.

"Don't do that," I said.

"Do what?"

"Talk about the future like that."

"Why not?" he asked. "It's what I see, and what I want."

"Yes, but it's not fair."

"I don't understand. What's not fair about it?"

I took a few shaky breaths. "It's not fair to make promises you don't know you can keep."

"What? I'm not making any—"

"You told Hope you'd bring Kayci with you tomorrow to see her, and you didn't even check with me." The shock on his face cut me, and I looked away so I'd remember why I was doing this. *He's too young,* I reminded myself. *I need to stop this now.* "You keep talking about the future as if it's happening, and all you're doing is getting both our hopes up and setting us up for disappointment."

"Maddie, I—"

"I never should have let you meet Hope, or let Hope play with Kayci. I know better than this. I should have let this be between you and me, and waited to see where this was going before introducing Hope to you."

"Maddie—"

"I should have—"

"Stop! Let me talk!" he said. "I don't understand why you need to have all these rules. It doesn't have to be this hard! I'm just asking for a simple relationship with you."

"Don't you understand? This *isn't* a simple relationship. I have to think about Hope's place in this, not just my own feelings. There's two of us to consider."

"You're thinking about this too hard."

"I'm not thinking about this hard enough!" I insisted. "I can't just think about how happy you make me. I have to think about how you'll fit into our already busy life. I have to think about what kind of dad you'll be to Hope. I have to think about what kind of husband you'll be to me. I have to think about whether we'll have more kids, and how Hope will feel about that."

"Maddie, you're getting way ahead of yourself. We haven't even slept together, and you're already thinking about our kids?"

"You don't get it!" I yelled. "You're only eighteen."

"So are you!"

"No, I'm nineteen, and I have a child. You have your whole life ahead of you. You're about to start college where you can go to frat parties and stay up all night doing stupid stuff. Me, I'll go to classes during the day and read bedtime stories to a toddler at night. I don't get a normal teenage life. If you stay with me, you won't either. I can't ask that of you."

"But you're *not* asking that of me," he said. "I'm here by choice. But before I can be a father to Hope and a husband to you, I'd like to try being your boyfriend."

I looked down at my hands. I couldn't say anything.

"Talk to me. Tell me what's going on."

"You don't understand."

"I'm *trying*," he said. "I don't know what you want. Tell me what you want, and I'll do it."

I looked at him. God, he was so beautiful. But he was so young. I felt like I was decades older, not just a year, and I couldn't let him give up his whole life to become a parent. That's what he'd have to be if he wanted to be with me, and I didn't believe he was ready for it.

"I want you to leave."

"What? No. Please. Stop trying to push me away."

"Jace," I said. I got up and walked over to him. I held out my hand, and he took it. He stood when I pulled him. "I care about you. But I don't think we're heading in the same direction."

"That's not what you said a few days ago," he protested.

"I was confused," I told him. Inside, my heart was breaking. But I knew this was the right thing to do. "I had a wonderful time that night, and I don't regret having met you. But I don't think we're meant to be together. It would be unfair to let this continue."

"You don't know what you're doing, Maddie."

"Jace, go home."

A Face From the Past

I couldn't look. I heard his wheels kick up the gravel as he made an angry departure, and was sure he'd turned onto the main road by the time I reached the front door.

I didn't have time to feel miserable; Hope's screaming filled the house. I rushed to her room to find Charlie holding her, a frustrated look on his face.

"What's wrong? Did she hurt herself?" I asked, taking her from his arms. He didn't answer, storming out of the room instead. Confused, I followed. Hope was still crying, but she was less frantic now that I was holding her.

"Charlie?"

He stopped and shook his head. "Is this how it's going to be now that you're dating?"

"What? I don't understand."

"I have a business to run. My wife is dying. I'm responsible for everyone and everything in this house. I do not have time to be a babysitter, as well."

I felt like the walls were caving in. He'd never spoken to me like this. I was hurt. I was ashamed. For the first time since I'd made this my home, I questioned whether I belonged here. Maybe I'd taken advantage of the Winstons' generosity for too long. Maybe this wasn't my family after all, but just a place I'd lived until I could take care of myself.

"You said you'd watch her," I said, looking down.

"You told me you'd be back before she woke up." He sighed. "I'm just tired, all right? I haven't gotten a lot of sleep these past few days, and I have a lot on my plate. I didn't mean to snap. I'll take her if there's something you need to do right now."

Hope was quiet now, sucking her fingers against my shoulder, but my pride was hurt. I'd be damned if I accepted any more help from him.

"It's fine. You don't need to do anything for me," I said. He drew his eyebrows together and I could see his apology coming. I didn't want to hear it. I grabbed my purse and keys.

"Maddie." I ignored him as I headed out the door, slamming it behind me.

As I stormed toward my car, I heard Fátima calling me. I kept walking, but she ran to catch up with me. Sighing, I turned.

"What?" I demanded angrily, even though she'd done nothing wrong.

"Mija, give me Hope," she said.

"What? No. I just need to get out of here. I'm taking her with me."

"No, mija. You're angry. You need to cool down. Let me take her so you can find peace."

"Why? Because I'm not capable of taking care of her myself?" I yelled. Even as I spun out of control, Fátima insisted, reaching out and taking Hope from my arms. I burst into tears.

"Oh, mija. What's wrong? Why are you so sad?"

"I'm making a mess of everything." I told her about my conversation with Jace, and how I let him go. Then I told her about Charlie.

"I don't belong here anymore. He doesn't want me. Nobody wants me."

"That's not true, mija. We are your family."

I shook my head. "No it's not. This is a household that took me in when I had no place else to go. These aren't my parents. My parents are in New Mexico, pretending they never had a daughter. I'm somebody's castoff, and now I'm the Winstons' charity case."

"You know that's not true," she said. Part of me knew I was being ridiculous. In all the time I'd been here, I'd never been treated like I was someone they felt sorry for. Charlie, Viola, and Fátima cared for me as if I were family. But I kept seeing Charlie's face. He'd made me feel like a burden he didn't want. He was an old man, and probably tired of having a whiny toddler around all the time.

I needed to find a way to move out, I just didn't know how. I'd become too dependent here. I wasn't sure I knew how to be on my own. I'd done a lousy job living on the streets before, now I was scared I'd go back to living like that. It was no place for Hope, or me.

"I need to go for a drive, and I want to take Hope with me."

"Not today," she said. I breathed through my nose, scowling at her. I knew she was right, but didn't want to give in. She put her hand on my arm. "You need a break."

"I need you to stop doing things for me!" I yelled. "Everyone around here is always doing things for me. I need to start doing things for myself!"

"Mija, that's not how family works. We help each other. Right now, you need help."

"I'm fine," I insisted.

"No. You need time to think," she told me. "I'll take Hope with me to get Señora Winston's pills, and then we go to my house. You pick her up there tonight."

"Fátima—"

"Mija," she warned. The conversation was over. I could see she wasn't going to budge. She gave me a hug, then walked away with my daughter. I watched as Hope clung to Fátima, feeling more alone than ever. Even my own daughter didn't want to be near me. I got in my car—another thing the Winstons gave me—and drove away.

I didn't know where I was going when I backed out of the garage. The tears started before I even left the gravel road. I was screaming by the time I reached the freeway. Without Hope in the car, I could release my emotions, but I also felt out of control. Driving was unsafe. I pulled off at the next exit, still sobbing as I parked. I couldn't understand what was wrong. Why did it feel like my life was falling apart? I should have felt happy, fulfilled, blessed, as my so-called religious mother would have said. I could have been living on the street, wondering where I'd find my next meal. Instead, I had everything I ever wanted, and was miserable. I'd thrown away a relationship with a guy who could have been perfect for me. Plus, I was waffling about a profitable career because it wasn't my dream job. I didn't even know what my dream job was.

"And now you're taking Viola from us!" I screamed at the God I never prayed to. I said it as if every good thing that came my way had been a curse, then I felt like a spoiled brat because I should have been nothing but grateful for the life I had. "I need to get out of here," I whispered. *Maybe if I found a different job, I could leave the Winstons and start over. I could take care of Hope and myself without any help from anyone.*

I got back on the road. I didn't know where I was going, but I was sure I'd recognize it when I found it. City scenery made way for waterways on both sides of the freeway, and the clouds stayed at bay, promising a warm afternoon with blue skies. I didn't care. I wished it was raining to match my storm inside. I drove in silence for forty minutes, then exited the freeway in Sausalito, taking the narrow street to the center of town, and parking in the lot near the docks. Once outside, I found comfort in the salty air and the sound of boats creaking against the dock. I walked on the wooden planks, letting the wind baptize me as I took in the scenery. The change was instant. I felt the dread and sorrow washing away from me, replaced by peace and acceptance.

I realized I couldn't leave the Winstons'. Not only was I being irrational, I didn't have the means to move out—not yet, at least. We'd all been under stress since Viola got sick. Her sudden turn and the doctor suggesting hospice made it clear she wouldn't be with us much longer.

Oh, God. Hospice. I'd forgotten they were coming to talk with Charlie today. No wonder he'd snapped. I felt like a total jerk. I'd only cared about my own feelings in that argument, never thinking about what he was going through.

I wanted to call him, but my pride wouldn't let me. I'd messed up badly and couldn't face him yet. *I'll talk to him when I go home.* I focused on other things to blur my guilt. As I looked at the glass sculptures in the art gallery window and the too expensive outfit in the boutique next door, I thought about what happened with Jace just a few hours earlier. *Was it a mistake?*

"No," I whispered. If it were different—if I didn't have a kid—I wouldn't have hesitated to dive into a relationship. Everything I knew about Jace so far made him seem to be the perfect guy for me. Okay, maybe not perfect. He'd choked when it came to Colton and his gang. But I got where he was coming from. Hell, I'd been an outcast the whole time I was in high school. It sucked. I would have loved to have been a part of the "in" crowd, accepted, have friends—even make-believe friends, like Jace was with Colton. No, that sounded awful. But it would have been nice to live a regular teenage life, and have regular friends and relationships. I was a mom, though, and I was starting to believe dating just wasn't going to happen while Hope was young. Guys my age weren't ready for a commitment with a girl who had a toddler at home. If I waited a few years, maybe then I could focus on romance. For now, I was fine being single, and Jace was better off finding someone who didn't have baggage with a bedtime.

I strolled past more art shops. My favorite was a portrait of a boy in a red robe, standing in a canoe in a river. The red stood out in contrast to the muted colors around him. I probably stared at it for ten minutes before moving on. I stopped at a pizza place and began to order at the counter, but a flashback of my last two dates with Jace interrupted my thoughts. I left and found a café instead. The place was different from The Apple Box. It was loud. The art shouted at me from the walls. The music competed with the noisy conversation around me. The barista behind the counter wore a bored look under her impressive amount of facial piercings.

This was the perfect place to be left alone.

I got coffee and a bagel before grabbing a table. It felt strange to sit by myself, without Hope. What had felt perfect just moments before suddenly felt awkward. I wasn't sure what to do, where to look, how to be. I sipped at my coffee, aware of my every move. Without someone in front of me, I felt like I was on display. I bit into my bagel, chewing slowly. Why was I here? Did I actually drive all the way to Sausalito to eat a bagel by myself in a crowded, obnoxious coffee shop?

I stared at the empty chair on the other side of the table. Then I pulled my phone out, scrolling through Facebook for a few minutes. That got boring fast. An abandoned newspaper lay on a vacant table nearby, and I grabbed it just to give myself something to focus on. I held it in front of me, but I didn't read any of the words. I knew I should be using this time to think, maybe come to terms with where I was in the moment, my breakup with Jace, my sorrow over Viola, my heartache over the fight I'd had with Charlie. But I didn't. Rather, I couldn't—this café was just too busy for any in-depth thinking. It was probably why it appealed to me in the first place.

Forget it. I sat back in my chair to people-watch. I spied on an elderly couple as they drank tea out of coffee mugs. When the woman dripped a little on her shirt, the man quickly got up and grabbed a few napkins. She lifted her chin while he dabbed at her shirt. Then he leaned down and kissed her. She smiled and patted his cheek before they went back to their tea. It was sweet, but after ending things with Jace, it also hurt to see. I turned and focused on another table occupied by a young couple around my age. He lifted his spoon of ice cream to her lips, and I immediately tried to find another table. I was surrounded by couples, a single person in a shop full of people in love.

I rolled my eyes at the absurdity of the situation. That's when I noticed a pair of legs sticking out from a table across the way. I looked at their owner—at his familiar slicked-back hair, his lopsided smirk, his lean and muscular body—and my stomach did a slow roll. I left my coffee and half-eaten bagel on the table and rushed out. I heard the door jingle after me, and didn't need to turn around to know he was following me. I yelped when his hand touched my shoulder and turned me around.

"Maddie?" Jordan asked. I caught my breath, and then glared at him. He laughed. "Maddie. It *is* you. Oh, my God. I thought I'd never see you again."

"Jordan," I said. Then I lifted my foot and stomped hard on his. Before he could react, I ran, weaving through the hallway of shops, aiming for the dock area where I'd parked my car. I heard him behind me, and I dug down to go faster. But he'd always been fast. Me, not so much. He caught me without effort, didn't even seem breathless when he spun me around again. I clenched my fists, ready to fight him if I needed to. I expected him to be furious. But he wasn't, not even a little. Instead, he looked amused.

"I guess I deserved that."

"You left me!" I yelled. I didn't care that people were staring at us.

"I panicked," he said. "I didn't know what to do. I was afraid they'd arrest me. And if they arrested me, I was going to jail. And then, well…" He paused, giving me a sheepish grin. "Well, they ended up arresting me, anyway. I was in jail for six months. By the time I got out, you were nowhere."

"Bullshit," I shot at him. "I don't believe you were arrested. They didn't have anything on you. I was the one who stole that woman's wallet. The most you would have gotten was a slap on the wrist."

"That's not true and you know it. I stole that guy's wallet on our way to San Francisco. I stole Jen's rent money. I wasn't sure what they'd have on me, and didn't want to take a chance. Plus, you were only sixteen and I was a legal adult. They would have pegged me for being an accomplice, for statutory rape, for driving without a license—"

"You were driving without a license?" I asked.

"Yeah, that's the first charge they got me on. The rent money and wallet followed later, plus possession. It was one officer's lucky day when they found me." He seemed so nonchalant about the whole thing, like it didn't even matter—like jail was something everyone did.

"Never mind. I don't even care. You left me, and you never looked back. I get it." I started to walk away, but he grabbed my hand. His touch went straight through me, flooding me with mixed emotions—anger, hurt, regret…and a dull ache, a wish that things had been different.

"I *did* look for you," he insisted.

"Really? Why didn't I see you? I looked for you, thinking maybe you'd have a heart and come back. But you left, and you forgot all about me."

"I never forgot you," he growled. He moved closer, and I felt my insides tighten. His face was tense, and I shrank back as he gripped my hand tighter. Realization crossed his face. "Sorry," he said, letting me go. He ran his hands through his hair, peering at the sky in embarrassment.

"Why'd you really leave?" I asked him. "I mean, before you were arrested. Why didn't you stay to help me?" He said nothing for a moment, and I braced myself to leave. All of this felt like a waste of time.

"I was scared," he finally said, and his words held me.

"Scared of getting caught? Or scared of raising a child?" I saw the look before he could hide it. I'd touched on something true.

"I wasn't scared of raising a kid," he said quickly. "I was scared of going to jail. I knew you could get around it. You're young and pretty. Your parents could help you out. I figured they'd pick you up, take you back home, and everything would be fine."

"Right. Everything would be fine." I shook my head at him. "You have no idea what I went through after you took off, do you?"

"Your parents didn't bail you out?"

"Oh, they got me out, all right. They even took me out to lunch and bought me a real meal. Then they bolted when I was in the bathroom. I never saw them again."

"Shit, babe, I'm so sorry. What did you do then?"

"I'm not your babe anymore." I glared at him. "I did the only thing I knew to do. I stayed in that parking lot."

"What?" The shock on his face made me angrier.

"You heard me. I slept on a pile of clothes behind the building. I scrounged for my food. I went weeks before I could get a hot shower. If it weren't for a few kind people who passed by, I would've starved."

"Why'd you stay?" he asked. "Why didn't you get help?"

"Because I didn't know how!" I yelled. "I didn't know anyone in this town. I was afraid if I left, I'd get lost and never find my way back. And I kept having this stupid hope you'd actually come back and find me."

"Are you…are you still living in the parking lot?"

"No, you dipshit," I said. "Do I look like I'm living in a parking lot?" He looked embarrassed. "I got a job with an elderly couple who took me in after three months. They helped me raise our daughter. They—"

"Our daughter?"

"Oh, yeah, you didn't know. Congratulations, it's a girl."

He looked so sad after I spat out the news, I had to remind myself I was angry with him. *Don't give in, Maddie. His interest in our child changes nothing.*

"We had a girl," he said. He gave a small laugh, though it sounded more like crying. "What's her name?"

"It's Hope, and you'll never meet her."

He breathed in, and then let the air out through his lips. "Hope," he whispered. He looked at me, and smiled. "It's a beautiful name." I nodded, but I didn't smile back. "So you're okay now?" he asked. "And Hope's okay?"

"We have everything we need," I told him.

"That's good." He looked at his feet in awkward silence. I needed to get out of there, get away from him, never see him again.

"Look, I'm going to leave," I said. "It was, uh, good to… I mean, take care, Jordan." I turned, but he stopped me with his hand on my arm.

"Wait," he said. I relented, staying when he moved his hand. "I messed up." I crossed my arms and let him continue. "I *was* scared. I didn't know if I'd be a good dad. I knew our kid would do great with you. You came from a good family, and you have a good heart. You even saw good in me, even though you deserved better than me. When they caught you, I ran because I was scared of getting caught. But after, when I knew I needed to go back for you, I kept running. The truth is, I never looked for you again. You didn't need someone like me in your life. Even after I got out of jail, I knew you'd be better off if I disappeared."

"Or you didn't want the responsibility of paying for another mouth to feed," I shot at him.

"No. It wasn't like that."

"I was pregnant, and you left me! You didn't even care! I had nowhere to go! I could have died. Our baby could have died!"

"I know that! I mean, I didn't think about it then. But now, I know. And I feel terrible about it. I wish I could take it all back, could have been there for you. But what would that have done for you? We were both homeless. I was out of options. We had no place to go, and I had nothing when I got out of jail. If I'd stuck around, you might not be in the spot you're in now."

He was right. He was the worst kind of jerk for leaving me and our unborn child. But if he hadn't, I never would have met the Winstons. I would have continued on the run with Jordan, raising Hope in an unstable situation. Life would be so much different.

"Can I at least see a picture of her?" he asked. I was ready to say no, but something in his face made me back down. He looked defeated. I realized he'd suffered from his decision to run, too. He gave up his chance to be a father. I might have been homeless for a few months, but he'd spent this whole time without Hope. He missed her birth, her first smile, the way she lit up when she saw someone she loved. He missed how good it felt to have her fall asleep on his chest. He missed everything about her. I would have relived those hard three months in the parking lot a thousand times just to be with Hope. He got a free life, I got her.

I got the better end of the deal.

"Please, Maddie. I won't ask for anything else." I sighed and gave in, opening my purse to pull out my phone. I scrolled through the photos until I found one, then handed the phone over. He took it and stared. His face softened and he swiped at his eyes.

"She looks just like you," he said, his voice breaking. "She's got your eyes, and your smile."

"Well, when she's not happy with me, she's all you," I told him. He laughed, wiping his eyes again before looking back at the photo. I found a few others and showed those to him. He kept saying how beautiful she was. I tried to remain closed off to him, to stay strong. I needed to go. Feelings I once had were resurfacing. If I didn't leave, I was going to forget why I hated him.

He handed me my phone, and I put it back in my purse. "I need to go," I said.

"Wait, I want to show you something."

No, I need to leave.

"What is it?"

"It's a surprise." He took my hand. "Trust me, you'll like it."

Permanent

I followed him back toward the shops. We got to the main street and he stopped in front of a tattoo parlor. There was no way to see inside, as the shop windows were mirrored and a heavy iron door guarded the entrance. The place was set apart from all the other shops, and the word TATTOO hung on the side of the building in large, menacing letters. It was the kind of place I avoided, and I felt intimidated being this close.

"You're getting another tattoo?" I asked, looking over his covered arms. He gave me an amused look.

"No, this is my place," he said.

"You own a tattoo parlor?" He'd had tattoos before I knew him. I'd also seen a few sketches he'd done just for fun. But I'd never known him to be a serious artist.

"Technically it's my buddy's shop, but I have a station here. I'm pretty good."

"Really?" I asked. He unlocked the door and opened it.

"Let me show you," he said. My eyes widened, and he laughed. "I mean, I have a portfolio. Come in and check it out."

He turned on the light as I followed him in. The floors were black and white, bordered by turquoise walls covered with photos and drawings of tattoos. Jordan led me to a chair in the back, and pulled out a binder.

"Here's some of the art I've done." My curiosity won out my nervousness, and I sat down to flip through the pages. I was amazed at what I saw—one beautiful piece of body art after another. Some were simple, like words on a forearm or a small flower on a foot, others were intricate and complex, like a half-body tattoo on the side of a woman or a full back tattoo on a man.

"I can't believe you do this," I told him, looking up from the book. "When did you learn how?"

"I've always known," he said. "I used to trade ink work with a few buddies before I got into the business. That's how I got all these tattoos."

"You never told me," I said, narrowing my eyes.

"It never came up," he said, shrugging. He offered a sly smile. "Have you ever thought about getting one?"

"No," I said quickly. It was a lie. Of course I'd thought about getting one. Ever since I could legally get a tattoo, I'd mused about what kind of ink I should get. Something small, for sure, and in a discreet area so I could hide it. Maybe a butterfly on my shoulder, or a few words on my inner arm. So far, I hadn't gone past thinking about possibilities. In reality, I was too chicken to put something permanent on my body.

"Come on, Maddie," Jordan said, nudging my hand with his. "I could give you something small. No one would have to know."

"I don't know. I really should be going. Hope's with Fa… She's with a sitter. I need to get her."

"It'll only take a few minutes. It'll be kind of like our secret, something to mark the end of us so we can move on."

As much as I wanted to say no, I liked the sound of that. The last few years had been wonderful with Hope. But they'd also been marked by pain. Today, I got the answers I needed about Jordan. I now knew where he'd been and why he never found me. Could he have made better choices and tried to find me? Sure. But we'd both made mistakes along the way. I was tired of being angry and ready to move forward. In a weird way, it seemed fitting to let him mark my body so I could close this chapter of my life.

"Okay, fine." He broke into a huge grin. "Let me see your book again so I can choose something."

"Nuh-uh," he said. "Let me surprise you." I gave him a look. "Trust me," he said for the second time. "I won't do anything you won't love."

"Fine," I said. I couldn't believe I was allowing him to this. "Can I at least choose where it's going?"

He placed his finger at my inner hip and I sucked in my breath at his touch.

"There," he said.

"Okay," I whispered.

I unbuttoned my pants as he put on gloves and got the gun ready. My hands were shaking as I tried to reveal the section of my hip where he'd pointed. I wasn't sure how I to do this without showing him every part he didn't get to see anymore.

"Here." He handed me a towel. "You'll have to pull your pants down, but this will cover you." I felt my heart pounding as I took the towel.

"I don't think this is a good idea," I said. He stopped what he was doing, put down the gun, and stripped off his gloves. Then he took my hand. His skin was warm and soft. His touch was somewhere in between something I knew and something I wanted to know. *No. I don't want to know this. I've already known this. This is a bad idea.*

"Do you trust me?" He looked steadily at me.

I used to.

"Yes," I said, closing my eyes. *This is reckless. I'm being totally stupid.* He placed the towel over my lower half, then grabbed my jeans by the hips and pulled them and my underwear down under the towel. I gasped at the motion, but kept my eyes closed. *What am I doing? What the hell am I doing?*

"Relax," he said. I nodded, but kept my eyes closed. I heard him snap on a new pair of gloves, then the buzz of the gun. He moved a portion of the towel to reveal my naked hip. I didn't want to see how much of my body he'd revealed. I figured he was doing his best to keep most of my groin covered, but I couldn't be sure. Everything in that area felt electrified, and I was afraid to open my eyes and reveal how turned on I was, and how much that scared me.

"This is going to sting, so brace yourself," he said. I held my breath, but he tapped my chest. "Breathe."

I exhaled as the needle touched my skin. It didn't hurt as much as I thought it would. I opened my eyes to watch him working on me, noting my modesty was still intact (though barely). His face was full of concentration. He paused and looked over at me.

"Don't watch," he said. "Let it be a surprise."

"I can't believe I'm letting you do this." I looked at the ceiling so I couldn't see the design. My hip was starting to burn where he was working, and I focused on breathing to keep from fidgeting.

"I'm almost done." His hand was on my thigh. I wasn't sure which was more distracting, the needle or his hand. My mind darted from his hand to the needle to my breathing. I hated that he was affecting me this way. I also loved it.

"Done," he finally said. "What do you think?" I peered at my hip as he put his tools away and stripped off his gloves. It was a small red heart with an infinity symbol through it.

"Really?" I asked. I couldn't help laughing. "Does this symbolize our relationship? Because that ended a while ago."

"Not really." he said while he washed his hands. He came back and leaned over me. I held my breath. I felt naked. I *was* naked, completely exposed to him. "We might not be together anymore, but we'll always have what we shared. Plus, there's a piece of you and me in our daughter. That's what's forever." He touched his lips to mine. I wanted to push him away, but didn't. Actually, I couldn't. With only a towel barely covering my lower half, any sudden movement would leave me completely exposed.

He moved his hand back to my hip, touching the area that hadn't been marked. "Do you like it?"

His eyes held me, and I couldn't look away from him. I wanted to, but I couldn't. I nodded. His hand made me dizzy as he traced my inner pelvis, coming dangerously close to a place no one had touched but him. I wanted him to stop. I was afraid he'd stop. I couldn't think. I couldn't breathe. I couldn't look at him. I closed my eyes, and shifted my hips. He took it as an invitation, and his fingers were suddenly inside me. I gasped and his mouth covered mine. He was gentle and commanding at the same time. I felt a familiar energy pulse from within, spreading through my body until it was coming out my pores. As much as I knew I should fight this—fight him—I couldn't help responding. Everything familiar about him came back to me. I knew his touch, his smell, his taste. I clung to him as

I peaked, crying out against his mouth. His fingers slowed but never left me, prolonging my orgasm as he'd learned how to do years before. He still knew me. And I still knew him.

"We belong together," he whispered. I couldn't argue. I didn't want to argue. I knew it was wrong. It felt wrong. But it also felt like everything I needed. "Give me another chance. We can be a family."

I closed my eyes, but not before the tears rolled down the sides of my face. A family—what I'd been wanting all this time. It was what he took away from me when he left. Since Hope was born, my visions of our perfect family of three were blurred by reality, but the dream never died. I now knew things wouldn't be perfect with Jordan. They never were. But I still loved him. I couldn't help but love him. He was a piece of my past I could hold on to; we could rebuild everything we'd lost in the last three years. Hope could get to know her father. She deserved a dad.

"Hey," he said, wiping my tears. "I'll never hurt you again. I promise. I've never stopped loving you. I want to make this right. Can we start over?"

I looked into his eyes. I'd always been fascinated by their color. When he was angry, they'd darken to a stormy blue. But now, they were calm and inviting, like the ocean's surface reflecting a flawless sky. With his pale features, his piercing gaze was electric. I nodded, and his face broke into a wide smile. He pulled me into his arms, and I winced as my hips moved.

"Sorry. We should get that bandaged up. You probably need to get out of here."

I glanced at the clock and grimaced. It was close to six, and I had a forty-five minute drive.

"Damn, I didn't realize how late it was." He applied a clear wrap to the tattoo and told me how to care for it. Because of its placement, there was no way I could put my tight jeans back on. He ran out of the shop and came back with a pair of his shorts from his car.

"You can get these back to me next time I see you," he said with a wink. My heart quickened when I realized what was going on. We were back together.

He busied himself at his station with his back to me so I could pull his shorts on, even though I could still feel the intimacy of his touch. Once dressed, he walked me back to my car.

"Dang, Maddie," he said when he saw what I was driving. "Looks like you haven't done so bad for yourself."

"It's just a Honda," I told him. "Charlie gave it to me for graduation."

"Charlie?" His eyes darkened and I recognized the glimmer of jealousy in his expression.

"Mr. Winston, the man who took me in."

"Oh," he said. "He must really care for you."

Before I got into the car, he traded phones with me so we could enter in each other's numbers. I flashed back to just a few days earlier, when Jace had done the same for me, and then brushed the thought away. Jordan handed my phone back to me, and put his in his pocket. Then he took my hand and pulled me close.

"I'll see you soon," he whispered, then lowered his mouth to mine. His kiss made me lightheaded, bringing me back to the secret moment we'd just shared.

I thought of that kiss the whole way back to Petaluma. As I pulled into Fátima's driveway, I couldn't help touching my fingers to my lips. *This is crazy.* Just that morning, I was breaking up with Jace and wondering if I'd ever have a normal love life. Now, I was back in a relationship with the man who gave me Hope, the promise of a real family on the horizon. It made sense, as crazy as it all was.

"Jordan," I said, testing his name on my lips.

Fátima gave me a curious look when I came to her door to get Hope. I knew she was wondering about the oversized shorts since most of the pants I wore were tight. I didn't explain.

"How was she?" I asked, following her into the house.

"Bueno," Fátima said. "She is eating dinner now. Are you hungry?"

I thought back to the partially eaten bagel and wasted cup of coffee. I was definitely hungry, especially when I smelled dinner cooking. Hope was in a booster seat and a fat Chihuahua sat underneath the table, waiting for scraps.

"Hey baby!" I said, and Hope's face lit up.

"Mama!" she cried. I gave her a few kisses on the cheek while she giggled. I sat down at the table, and Fátima placed a plate of tamales in front of me. As I ate, she told me about their day of fun. She'd taken Hope on a walk to feed the ducks at Lucchesi Park and let her play at the playground.

"Hope kept asking about KK. What is KK?" she asked. My cheeks burned at this, but I shrugged as if I had no idea.

We cleared our plates in no time. Fátima got up to get us more, but I stopped her.

"I need to get back. Charlie will be going to bed soon, and I want to talk with him." She nodded.

"He loves you, mija."

"I know," I agreed. "He's under a lot of stress. And I… I wasn't in a good place this morning."

"Are you better?" she asked. An involuntary flutter traveled through me.

"Yes," I said, thinking about the afternoon. "I think I needed a drive and some time away to look at things differently." I didn't want to tell her about Jordan yet. She knew about him—I'd told her enough that any mention of our reunion would be alarming. I needed to break the news, but I wanted to get used to the idea first.

We got Hope cleaned up, and she walked us out to the car, pushing a bag of tamales into my hand.

"For Señor Winston," she said, though the weight told me there was enough in the bag to feed all of us for a couple of days.

"Thank you, Fátima, for everything."

"Mija, it's what family does."

***

Back home, I juggled my sleeping toddler as I opened the door. Charlie was reading on the couch when I walked in.

"Let me help you," he said, getting up. I knew this was his way of apologizing, and I smiled, letting him know we were okay. He led the way to Hope's room. I didn't bother to undress her; keeping her asleep was more important. She was out, and I wanted her to stay that way all night.

Once out of her room, Charlie gave me a hug.

"I'm so sorry I snapped at you," he said. I held onto him for a moment.

"You don't have to be sorry. You're under so much stress with Viola. I forgot you were meeting with hospice today, and feel terrible about that. How did it go?"

"It was okay," he said. "It's hard to admit she's dying. The people who came were really nice. We set up a care schedule, and they're here to support us, too. I didn't quite understand what hospice does; I saw it as a death sentence for Viola."

"Will we be able to start working together again?"

"I think you have a good start on what you're learning," he answered. "Why don't you enjoy your vacation before school starts? I think Hope would rather you spend time with her than being out in the fields."

"Thank you," I said, giving him a hug. Getting some time to relax work in Viola's garden would be great, but mostly I was thinking about spending more time in

Sausalito with Jordan, and letting him get to know his daughter.

"I thought you might want to spend more time with that boy you're dating," Charlie said. I looked at him sharply, thinking he was referring to Jordan. Then I realized he meant Jace. "When will I get to meet him?"

"One day," I said, avoiding his gaze. I felt bad for lying. But what could I tell him? *I broke up with Jace and I'm suddenly back together with the guy who took off on Hope and me.* I pushed the thought out of my head as quickly as it came. This was crazy. But love wasn't supposed to make sense, right? Besides, everyone deserved a second chance.

"How's Viola?" I asked.

"She slept all day, but her fever's gone." His expression drooped, and I felt bad for bringing it up.

"Maybe she just needed rest," I said, but we both knew it was more than that. He nodded, playing along with me.

"Probably," he said. He placed a kiss on my forehead. "I should go to bed. It's been a long day."

"Same," I told him. I had so much to process, and I needed the space to do it.

Once I closed my door, I tugged down the waist of Jordan's shorts over my hip so I could see the tattoo, lifting a corner of the bandage. The tattoo was shiny with ointment, making the red and black stand out against my pale skin. The area was reddened and tender to the touch, but nothing too bad. I liked the way it looked. It made me feel like a badass. I stuck the bandage down again, then changed into my sweats for bed. I looked at my phone to see if there were any message from Jordan. Instead, I saw Jace's name.

If this had been earlier, even after breaking things off with him, just seeing his name would have made me smile. Instead, I frowned. I was glad I broke up with him when I did, but I still had some regret. He was a good guy. He would have been good to Hope. But now that Jordan was back in the picture. I had to see that through.

I thought about deleting Jace's text without reading it, but I was curious.

Jace: *I'm not giving up on you. I know you have a lot going on right now, but I think you made a mistake. I'll respect your space and your boundaries, but I'm not going away. For the next month, I'm texting you a reason why I like like you.*

As I was reading, another text came through.

Jace: *Reason #1. You look cute even with a pee stain on your shirt.*

I tried to close myself off from him, to avoid letting his text affect me, but it was too late. I thought back to that day at The Apple Box. I figured he'd been judging me, like the barista. Apparently he was only checking me out.

"It's over," I reminded myself. I moved to delete, but hesitated. I read the first text again: *I'm not giving up on you....* I closed out of his text and pulled up Jordan's name on my phone.

Me: *Hey.*

I stared at my phone for a few minutes, waiting for his text. It marked that he'd read it, followed by three dots.

Jordan: *Hey yourself, beautiful.*

I couldn't come up with anything clever to say. Why was this so awkward? I'd known him for years, but now I was feeling like a total dork around him.

Me: *So, today was something, wasn't it?*

Jordan: *I think it was pretty special.*

Me: *Oh? How so?*

I was being coy, but I just needed to see how he felt about what had happened.

Jordan: *Well, I got some coffee and the barista gave me a free add shot of espresso.*

Me: *Jordan!*

Jordan: *Oh yeah, and I reconnected with this sweet little thing I haven't stopped thinking about for the past few years.*

I closed my eyes, feeling my insides warm. Then I texted back.

Me: *Tell me more…*

Jordan: *I'd rather show you. What are you doing tomorrow?*

Me: *Nothing. But I have Hope….*

There was a pause in his texting. My text showed that he read it, but he didn't start typing back right away. I put the phone on the bed and went to brush my teeth. As I was spitting out the toothpaste, I heard my phone ding. I rinsed my toothbrush, and then pounced on the phone.

Jordan: *Let's all go out. I want to meet her. We can go grab a slice of pizza.*

What was it about pizza?

Me: *I'm not really all that into pizza. Let's go someplace else. Where should I meet you?*

Jordan: *Come pick me up at my place. I live in San Rafael. We'll decide when you get here.*

He texted his address.

Me: *I'm glad I saw you today. I can't wait to see you tomorrow.*

Jordan: *Same here. Goodnight, beautiful.*

Me: *Goodnight.*

Daddy's Girl

I pulled into Jordan's neighborhood, and scanned the street for his address. The houses were similar to the ones Jordan lived near back home. They didn't have the same southwestern style, but appeared worn and uncared for. Bikes and toys littered weed-filled front yards. Paint was peeling off walls. "Beware of Dog" signs were posted on multiple fences. It was a huge difference from where I lived in Petaluma—a large Mediterranean-style home, beautifully landscaped out front, and rows of vineyards behind. I felt repulsed by his rundown neighborhood.

"You were living in a parking lot three years ago," I reminded myself aloud, even as I realized my homeless past was the exact reason why I didn't want to be here. I didn't ever want to live like this. *You could be living here, though. If it weren't for Charlie and Viola, you'd probably still be homeless.*

I looked in the rear view mirror at Hope. She was quietly staring out the window. I knew she wasn't aware of any difference between our life of privilege and one that included homes like these. Part of me wanted to shield her from this. I was tempted to turn around and forget this whole thing. Jordan only knew my phone number, not how to find me. I could disappear and be done with him for good, returning to my comfortable life.

The other part of me kept my hands on the wheel and my eyes searching for Jordan's house. *Hope deserves to know her father,* I reminded myself. Besides, a sheltered life would do her no good.

I saw him before he saw me. He was on the steps of a white house, its front path bordered by dirt. There were dead rosebushes in front of the porch, judging by the withered brown foliage. I mentally thought of ways I could revive the front yard of this home, starting with plants that could replace the dying bushes. This made me laugh. Years earlier, I'd been foolish enough to believe we could leave Gallup, penniless, and move right into our dream house. Man, had I been wrong about that. Yet, here I was, practically planning another dream house when we'd only just reconnected.

Jordan was staring at his phone when I pulled up. I watched him for the few seconds he didn't notice me, noting the things that had drawn me in when I saw him for the first time. I also noted what that had changed. He was older now: it was both strange and enticing to see the difference in his posture, his leaner face, and his sculpted arms and chest. I hadn't realized how young we were back then. I wondered if I had changed in his eyes, too.

He looked up and smiled, and I felt my heart jump. I shook my head at this, amused. I'd been mad at him for so long, yet he could melt me with a smile. I took in his slicked-back hair, the way his white T-shirt clung to his chest, the tattoos covering his arms, the tightness of his jeans, his bare feet… Yeah, he'd grown into a man.

When he reached the car, he glanced at the back seat, taking his first look at our daughter. She had no idea who he was, peering out the window at him, then looking away when she realized he was watching her. I could see her shyness winning out. I studied his expression and warmed when I saw his face soften. He got in the car, and I smelled the cigarette he'd just smoked.

"You still smoke." He shrugged, then kissed me. My heart fluttered at the casual way he did it, as if we'd never been apart. He turned around. Hope was watching him, but turned her face away when he looked at her.

"Hi, Hope, baby. I'm your daddy," he said. All my warm feelings were suddenly gone, and I tensed up. She probably had no idea what he meant, but I was bothered by the way he blurted it out. When he looked at me, he saw I was upset. "What's wrong?"

"I thought we'd ease into telling her about you."

"She doesn't know about me?"

"Well, no. She turns three in October. She's too young to understand why she doesn't have a dad."

"You haven't told her anything about me?"

I felt my insides boil. The emotions I'd stuffed down resurfaced.

What should I have told her?" I asked, glaring.

"Whoa there, Maddie," he said, holding his hands up. "I just asked a question. I didn't realize she knew nothing about me. It makes sense. We'll take things slow so she can get to know me, okay?"

I nodded, taking a deep breath as I simmered down. Then I rolled my eyes.

"Sorry," I said. "I guess I get a little protective of her."

"It's because you're a good mom." He squeezed my hand, then laced his fingers through mine. "You don't have to do this alone anymore. I want to help, to be a part of your lives. We can be a family."

I loved the way that sounded.

He directed me toward the restaurant he'd chosen, some place called Sol Food. He said they served Puerto Rican food, which he described as simple Spanish-style cooking. I'd never had it, and he insisted I'd love it.

"What about Hope?" I planned to feed her from my plate, but I knew how picky she was. "Is it spicy?"

"Not at all," he said. "Trust me, she'll like it."

We found parking and walked a few blocks to the restaurant. I carried Hope, and she kept her face hidden so Jordan couldn't see her. I felt her peek at him every few minutes to see if he was paying attention. When we got to the restaurant, there was a line out the door.

"Everyone goes here," Jordan explained. "Don't worry, the line moves fast." Sure enough, we were in the door after only fifteen minutes. We ordered at the counter, and he paid while I found a table. It was family-style seating, and I saw a spot with space for three toward the back. There were no booster seats, and Hope was too big for the tiny highchair in the corner, so I hoped for the best as I placed her on the bench next to me.

"Be a big girl and stay with me, okay?" She stayed, but I wondered how long it would last. Sol Food was different from the other places I'd taken her. Usually we were with Charlie who preferred quiet restaurants. Hope knew how to behave in a restaurant, though her booster seat and Charlie's reproachful stare helped keep her in line. Here, she had the freedom to run all over the place once she figured out nothing was holding her back. I prepared myself for a disastrous meal, sure I'd spend it chasing her. Still, I was drawn to the energy here. Loud Spanish music played through the speakers, and the kitchen staff was louder. Even the walls were loud, painted a wild orange color and covered in a mess of art. The atmosphere was frenzied, but casual about it. It seemed like everyone knew everyone; I saw people hop from one table to the next, visiting with friends.

Jordan joined us, and the waiter followed, setting water down in front of Jordan and me, and a bowl of sticky bananas in front of Hope. I moved them before she could grab them.

"Mine!" she cried. If we'd been in one of Charlie's regular restaurants, her voice would have caused everyone to look at us. Here, however, her voice blended into the noise.

"They're sweet plantains," Jordan said. "They're kind of like a dessert. She'll love them."

I didn't want her hands to get messy, so I cut one large plantain in half and speared it with my fork. I took a nibble off the side and was surprised by how delicious it was. It tasted like banana, but better and more sugary than what I usually gave her, especially before dinner.

"Me, Mama," she said, opening her mouth like a little bird. I put the rest of the piece in her mouth, and she happily chewed it. "More," she demanded, and opened her mouth again. Jordan laughed as I continued to feed her tiny pieces.

"See, I told you she'd like it." I handed him the fork, and was amused by the discomfort on his face. "She'll warm up to you faster if you're the one feeding her," I explained. "Just make sure the pieces are small so she doesn't choke, and to make it last longer."

He nodded, and took one small piece off a banana. Timidly, he brought it to her mouth. Hope accepted it without question, chewing it and then opening her mouth for more.

"It's almost like feeding a dog," he joked.

"Something like that."

By the time our food arrived, Hope was infatuated with Jordan. It didn't hurt that he was doing his best to make her laugh, and succeeding. I could tell he was loved her attention, eating up the way she watched everything he did. When we started to eat, she refused the food on my plate, more interested in what Jordan had on his. My heart expanded as he fed our daughter, taking turns with each bite to give her some of his rice and chicken. He wasn't even worried about germs, casually sharing the same fork.

He was also right about Puerto Rican food. I decided I could eat like this every day. I liked the infectious commotion. It was so much better than the stuffy places Charlie took us.

"What now?" I asked as we headed back to my car. I knew I'd eaten too much by how tight the waistband of my jeans was. I didn't care. I'd do it again in a heartbeat…at least, after I digested a bit.

"Think she can handle a movie?" he asked. I shook my head. There was no way. We'd managed to keep her sitting for more than an hour at the restaurant. To get her to sit for another two hours would be nearly impossible.

"I doubt it."

"Well, let's try anyway," he said. "If it doesn't work out, we can leave."

"Okay," I agreed, though I foresaw this ending in disaster.

We were lucky, though. The movie we chose was a kid's movie that had been out for weeks. Apparently, we were the only family in town who hadn't seen it; the theater was empty. Hope didn't even last through the opening previews before she was running up and down the row we were sitting in. I wondered whether we should give in and leave when Jordan leaned over.

"Let her play," he said, taking my hand. "It's not like she's bothering anyone."

He was right. We had an empty theater and a chance to relax for two hours while she kept running away, and then coming back to us. I settled into my seat, keeping one eye on the screen and the other on my giggling daughter, all while aware of Jordan's hand. Hope eventually noticed the animated trolls on the screen, and came to sit next to me. That lasted a few minutes before she climbed over her seat to sit in my lap. She played with my arm as she stared at the screen, and Jordan let go of my hand to play with hers. I waited to see how she'd react. She didn't even flinch, but curled her hand around his fingers, her eyes still on the screen. I had no words for how this felt, watching my daughter hold her father's hand. I felt her breathing get slower and her body relax. Soon she was sleeping against me, her hand still in Jordan's, me snuggled between the two of them. I looked over and saw him watching her. His eyes moved from her to me, and he gave me a goofy grin.

"I didn't...I didn't know," he said. He looked away quickly, and I knew what he was feeling. He didn't know it was possible to fall in love at first sight like this. He didn't know what it was like to have a daughter. I thought back to the months before he left, and how distant he'd been about the pregnancy. We'd hardly talked about plans for after the baby was born, and only when I started the conversation. We didn't even discuss names. I'd been in denial back then, but now I knew—the thought of being a dad had terrified him.

"You couldn't have," I said. I moved my hand slowly from under Hope and rested it on his shoulder. He turned back to me, eyes glistening. He gave a small laugh and swiped at his eyes. He opened his mouth to say something, then closed it and shook his head. Instead, he placed his hand on the side of my cheek and kissed me. His lips were soft, and he flicked my tongue with his in a gentle tease. I forgot the movie as he leaned back and looked into my eyes.

"I'm sorry I left you," he said. "Please tell me about what happened, and don't leave anything out."

I looked down, hesitating before I returned to a place I never wanted to be again, a time when no one wanted me—not my parents, not the people who averted their eyes as they passed me, and not Jordan. Everything I'd owned was in Jordan's car: my clothes, my journal, money… Everything. Stealing that woman's wallet got me arrested, and Jordan vanished.

"That first night in jail was the best sleep I'd get in a while," I said. "I didn't know it at the time. My parents came to get me the next day. When I saw the cold way my dad was looking at me, I wanted to crawl back into my cell.

They took me out to lunch, and he finally let me have it. He told me, 'We didn't raise you this way,' and I snapped."

I stopped my story to wipe away the tears I didn't even know had started. It seemed silly that the movie was playing while I was talking, singing and dancing on the screen while I relived the worst months of my life. "I reminded him how he'd kicked me out when I turned up pregnant—the moment I needed him most. I reminded him that I had nothing, and no other way to survive. I reminded him that instead of being my father, he chose to treat me as if I were a stranger."

I stopped talking, choking on my tears. My father had always been stern. He raised me according to his military background, and expected me to conform. When I got pregnant, I hid it as long as I could. Even knowing how strict he was, I never expected him to throw me out. When I could no longer hide the truth, he told me to leave. He barely gave me enough time to pack. I left with the clothes I was wearing, a few things in a bag, and a small amount of cash my mom slipped in my hand. For him to come down hard on me for stealing when I had no other way was unfair and cruel. I'd never stood up for myself to my dad. No one could. But on that day, I couldn't let him believe he was right.

Jordan put his arm around my shoulder as I cried. He kissed my forehead. "I'm so sorry," he said. I shook my head, pushing him away so I could continue.

"He left me there. At the restaurant. I'd gone to the bathroom, and when I came back, he and my mother were gone. I ran out as they were getting in the car. I screamed for them to stop, but they didn't. I had no one. You were gone. My parents were gone. I didn't know where I was or how to get help. I had no friends I could call. I was on my own, and I had no idea how to take care of myself."

The next few months were my personal hell. The shame. The penetrating cold. The wind that blew all night long, even as I tried to find relief under my flimsy blanket. It seemed so long ago, and yet, it could have been yesterday the way the memories returned. I felt the raw hunger in my belly, the kind that made me ravenous and nauseous at the same time. I could even feel the sheer exhaustion of sleeping with one eye open, unsure if that night would be the one when some human predator would see me as their prey.

Back then, sores covered my body from frequent scratching. Without a regular way to bathe, I knew I smelled bad, but I'd gone nose-blind to the stench after a few weeks. Simple things I'd taken for granted—changing clothes, using a toilet, seeing my reflection in the mirror— all became luxuries I couldn't afford. I'd never known loneliness like that. My only friend was the old man who shared the same corner of the parking lot, and he hardly spoke. There were days when no one looked at me, and I wondered if I even existed anymore. I wasn't sure if my parents thought of me at all, or how they explained me away to anyone who asked where I was. My friends had probably long forgotten me.

And Jordan? I figured he was several states away, erasing my memory as he lived a free life. Still, at least in those first weeks, I hoped that he'd come back for me. I knew I'd find help if I left the parking lot, but was afraid I'd miss him if he came back to look for me. So I stayed. By the time I realized he was gone for good, I'd found a job with the Winstons. Besides, I hadn't known where to look for help.

All the while, Jordan stroked the back of my neck. It felt strange to tell him of the first night in the parking lot, the night I was sure he'd come back for me, while he was here comforting me. I felt torn between slapping his hand away and telling him to leave, and folding myself in his arms. I chose to do nothing, letting his simple gesture be comfort enough as I told him how I met the Winstons a few days later and began working for them.

"I was three months into the job when I went into labor." Jordan's hand stilled at my neck as I described giving birth to Hope in the vineyard. "After she was born, I realized I had nothing to give her."

"You had the Winstons." I shook my head.

"At that point they were just my employers. I was still sleeping in the parking lot on a pile of clothes, and used blankets from the donation truck across the lot to keep warm. I was starting to get used to that kind of life. But when I held Hope, I realized she didn't deserve that kind of life. I might have accepted homelessness, but I couldn't accept that for my daughter. So…" I trailed off. *Will he understand what I did? Will he hate me for it?*

"So?" he asked. I took a deep breath.

"So, I gave her up."

The animated trolls on the movie screen continued their song and dance to the near-empty theater. Their celebration was a sharp contrast to Jordan's face.

"You gave her *up*? You mean, *for adoption*?" He looked down at our sleeping daughter. "I don't understand. She's here with you now."

"That's because the Winstons helped me get her back. I'd heard once that mothers could take their babies to fire stations if they were unable to keep the child, and no one would ask any questions. So I did that. I took her to the fire station near the Winstons' house and left Hope with the fireman on duty. As I walked back to the house, I realized what I'd done. Charlie found me crying on the road, and took me back to the house. He and Viola invited me to live with them, and they helped me to get Hope back. They've been taking care of us ever since."

Jordan was quiet. His hand had left my neck, and he was staring at Hope. I didn't know what he was thinking. He reached over to her and touched her little hand. Even in her sleep, she grasped his finger again. He smiled, and then he looked at me.

"I'm so sorry you had to go through all this alone. Now that I've met her, I can't imagine what it must have felt like to let her go."

"It was the hardest thing I've ever done, but I felt like I had no other choice. I wanted her to have more than I could give her. Thankfully, Charlie and Viola offered to help and gave me a way to be her mother."

The sharp trill of my phone interrupted our conversation, sounding almost louder than the song on the screen. Hope remained asleep in my arms, preventing me from moving

"Can you reach that?" I asked, gesturing toward my purse. "Go ahead and take it out." He grabbed my phone and handed it to me. I recognized the home number. "Thank God no one is in here." I laughed as I answered it.

"Maddie? You need to come home," Fátima said. I heard sadness in her voice, and my chest tightened.

"Viola? Is she…"

Fatima sighed, and I knew the answer before she said it. "Señora Winston está muerta."

Viola had died.

I closed my eyes. Knowing this was coming didn't make it easier. I remembered the first time I saw Viola, her delicate features masked by the scarf on her head and large sunglasses. She'd noticed me first, Charlie later told me. I reminded them of their late daughter, and they were determined to find some way to help me. If she hadn't seen me, I don't know if I would have survived.

"Maddie?" I opened my eyes.

"I'm on my way." I hung up, feeling numb. The movie blared. The trolls sang, and it seemed so out of place, so stupid. I looked down at Hope sprawled across me. I wasn't sure how to get up.

"Who was that?" Jordan asked. "What's wrong?"

I took a deep breath.

"Viola." I wanted to cry. I wanted to be alone. I didn't know how to react. "She just passed away. I need to go home." Then I realized I was Jordan's ride. "Uh, you can come with me, I guess." I knew this wouldn't go over well. I hadn't figured out how to tell Charlie that Jordan and I were together again, and this definitely wasn't the right time, but all I could think about was getting home quickly, and Jordan's house was in the opposite direction.

"Don't worry about me," he said, picking my purse up from the ground as I shifted Hope. She whimpered, and I shushed her. "I can call one of my roommates. You need to be with your family, and I don't want to get in the way."

I gave him a grateful smile as Hope started to cry. We left the theater, the lobby blissfully quiet in contrast with the noisy movie. Jordan walked behind me, still carrying my purse as Hope wailed. He followed me to my car, and stood by as I put her in the car seat.

"Shush, baby. We'll be home soon." I took Hope's sippy cup from the diaper bag and handed it to her, but she pushed it away. It would be a long drive home.

"I'm really sorry about that lady," Jordan said, hugging me. I wanted to cry, but not here. He placed his hand on my cheek as he kissed me. I was anxious to leave, but he left his lips pressed against mine. "I'm so glad I found you again," he said. I wished I could be in the moment with him, but my mind was with Viola.

"Me too," I said, pulling away and putting my hand on the door. When he tried to kiss me again, I turned my head. He brushed his lips against my cheek.

"You have to go, I know. I'm sorry. It's just hard knowing I can't be with you and Hope all the time. Maybe we can hang out tomorrow?"

"I can't," I said. I noticed disappointment on his face. "I need to be there for my family," I explained. I knew he didn't understand how much Viola meant to me. He couldn't.

"Right. Sorry," he apologized again. "I'll text you later to see how you're doing." I nodded, and got in the car. I glanced at the rearview mirror as I drove away, seeing him walk in the opposite direction. The phone was to his ear, probably calling for a ride home.

I didn't cry on the way home, thinking of Viola as I drove. I recalled the times she'd mothered me in those first few months, and how much she'd loved Hope. As her mind slipped, her friendship with Hope deepened. I thought back to the last time they were in the garden, playing with blocks as I dug in the dirt. In the time I'd known her, our roles reversed. She went from motherly to childlike. I was grateful I'd been able to give back to her in her final months, nurturing her as she'd once nurtured me.

Bird

My phone pinged in my pocket as I put Hope to bed that night. I ignored the text for the time being, and watched as she curled onto her side in her sleep.

It had been a long night.

When I'd gotten home, I broke down seeing Charlie hold Viola's lifeless hand. He comforted me as I cried, even though I knew he was suffering more than I was. We sat with her, telling her how much she meant to us. A hospice worker stayed with us as we mourned, allowing us to say our goodbyes before she called the funeral home.

I closed Hope's door and pulled out my phone as I headed to my bedroom.

Jace: *Reason #2. You always make sure your family comes first.*

I was expecting Jordan to text, and Jace's message caught me off guard. I swore I wouldn't call him, but I needed a friend who understood.

"Hey," he said in the phone. I noted the surprise in his voice.

"Hey." *I shouldn't have called.* "Viola died." I didn't sugarcoat it, opting to rip the Band-Aid off immediately. I heard him suck in his breath.

"Oh, Maddie. I'm so sorry."

I burst into tears. He said nothing as I cried, and I was thankful for that. The last thing I needed were meaningless words, like, "It's going to be okay," or "At least she's not hurting anymore." His silence offered more comfort than words ever could. I needed someone to be there and not try to fix the unfixable.

"I should go," I said when I could finally catch my breath. "I'm sorry I called you."

"Wait," he said. "Don't go. You can go back to not talking to me tomorrow. Tonight, let me be there for you."

It was exactly what I needed him to say. I began talking about Viola, sharing all the things I was going to miss about her. He simply listened, offering only a few murmured affirmations. I cried a little more, but spoke through the tears. By the end, my emotions were raw, but my heart felt light.

"Are you going to be okay?" he asked. "I can come over, if you need a friend right now. No strings, I promise."

It sounded tempting, and I felt guilty as I realized I wanted to say yes.

"I don't think that's a good idea," I said.

"I don't understand what went wrong."

"Jace—"

"No, hear me out. We were good together. You didn't even give it time to see that. We were good together, and we could still be good together."

"I'm seeing someone," I blurted out. Then I held my breath. He didn't speak. "Jace?"

"I'm here," he said. He was silent again, but this time I heard him breathing. "How long has this been going on?"

"It just happened. I know this sounds strange, but—"

"Yeah, it sounds strange," he cut in. "We had an amazing couple of dates together before you broke things off. And now, all of a sudden, you're seeing someone? I don't get it. You claim you couldn't trust me even though I was doing everything to show you could. But then some new guy comes along and takes my place. What does he have that I don't?"

"He's Hope's father."

I heard the phone drop, or maybe he threw it.

"Goddammit!" I heard in the background. I considered hanging up, but I stayed on the line. I heard fumbling noises on his end of the line, and then he was back.

"What are you even thinking, Maddie?" he demanded.

"This isn't your concern."

"You're right. But you're also out of your damn mind. How is this a good idea?"

"I don't have to answer to you!" I shouted. "I ran into him the other day. He's changed. He wants us to be a family."

"He lost his right to be a family with you when he left you."

"You don't understand! He was scared! Plus…" I stopped myself before I told him Jordan had been in jail. All of this was bad enough.

"And that makes it right?" Jace asked. "Weren't you scared, too? You were only sixteen, and yet you didn't walk out on Hope. You stuck around and made it work."

Of course, he'd think that. He didn't know the whole story. He didn't know Jordan and I were similar. We both gave up on Hope when things got scary and hard. I got my second chance. Now it was Jordan's turn.

"He's here now," I told him. I felt my heart beat a little faster as I considered the words that would end it all. Finally, I said them. "I'm still in love with him."

He didn't speak. There was silence for a few seconds, and then I heard a click. He hung up on me. I angrily moved to plug the phone in for the night when I noticed a text notification.

Jordan: *Hey, babe. Been thinking of you all night. Hope you're okay. Sweet dreams.*

I looked at it for a moment, not sure how to feel. It wasn't an invitation to talk, or even to continue the conversation. I typed back, hoping I was wrong.

Me: *I've been thinking of you, too. It's been a rough night. Tomorrow we plan the funeral.*

Jordan: *Hang in there. xoxo*

I frowned. He was definitely not into talking. Not that I was in the mood, but I needed him to be more interested in how I was doing. My phone pinged again, but this time the text wasn't from Jordan.

Jace: *I don't understand how you can love someone who left you when you needed him most. He failed you in the worst way, and he doesn't deserve a second chance. If you think you can't do this without him, you're wrong. Millions of moms have managed to raise happy kids when the dad chose to walk out, my mom included. You don't need him.*

I was tempted to respond. I wanted so badly to tell him he was wrong, but part of me was afraid he wasn't. My phone vibrated in my hand, and I read his next text.

Jace: *What does Charlie think about your new relationship?*

I threw my phone on my bed and glared at it. Then I picked it up and started typing.

Me: *Goodbye, Jace.*

I turned the phone off so I couldn't receive any more texts.

I didn't sleep well that night. My mind was going wild, my thoughts swirling. Every time I started to drift, they attacked me again. My grief over Viola's passing. Jace's hurt expression when I saw him leave. Jordan's taillights as he left me behind with the cops. The way Jordan touched me after the tattoo. How I shouldn't love someone who'd betrayed me. How I wasn't sure this was love, or just a desire to be a family. Every word of my texts with Jace. My urge to turn my phone back on and tell him off for everything he said. My urge to apologize and try to make things right. My urge to get Jordan to say the right things and be there for me. My wish that no one had to die, ever, and we could all be happy forever. My wish that life didn't have to be so messy.

I woke up the next morning with a headache and my stomach on edge. For a moment, I didn't remember anything. Then it all came back. My heart ached at the thought of Viola's empty room. Today, Charlie and I would go over funeral arrangements. I dreaded it, but didn't want him to do it alone.

I reached for my phone and turned it on. I expected a barrage of texts from Jace, and hoped for a morning greeting from Jordan. My phone was silent. No new messages. Frowning, I got up and took a shower. I kept my phone away from me as I dried off and got dressed. Only when my hair was dry did I check my phone again. No new messages.

Charlie was standing at the sink, staring out the window when I came into the kitchen. He turned and gave me a small smile. I noted the dark circles under his eyes.

"You didn't sleep well, either?" I asked. He gave a light laugh.

"Is it that obvious?" I shook my head, though it was a lie. "Sorry you couldn't sleep. Maybe tonight will be better."

"Maybe," I said. I moved toward him, and he put his arm around my shoulder, kissing the top of my head. Even after losing his wife, he still showed me love.

A bird landed on a branch of the tree outside the window. It preened its yellow feathers, then hopped a little further down the branch before turning to face us. We watched as it cocked its tiny head, then flew away.

"Bird," Charlie whispered, and I felt him shake.

"Do you remember the day you and Viola asked me to live with you?" I asked. He nodded, wiping his eyes. "I remember looking out the window and seeing a bird just like that one looking back at me. It was when I knew I was home." I paused, and wrapped my arms around his waist as he held on to me. "Maybe now Viola is a bird," I said. "She's probably watching us, wondering why we're so sad when she's so happy."

"She was always so happy," Charlie whispered.

"Yes, but now she's home," I told him.

I didn't know if there was an afterlife. My mother claimed there was and prayed for those who'd never get to Heaven. But then, her idea of Heaven allowed people like her and my father in, but kept out good people who didn't pray like them. In my version of Heaven—if there was a Heaven—we lived forever as our favorite things. I'd probably be the wind, traveling around the world in flurried gusts. But Viola? She most definitely was a bird.

Hope woke up an hour later, after Charlie and I had most of Viola's funeral planned. It would be three days from now at St. Andrew's Church, followed by a catered lunch in our home. Charlie had an obituary written, one he'd been working on for days. I read it over, tearing up as I saw that he referred to me as their daughter.

"I hope that's okay," he said. I nodded, unable to say anything through my tears. It meant more to me than he'd ever know. We filled in the missing information, and he gave me instructions on how to submit it to the newspaper.

"Once everything dies down, we can talk about where to spread her ashes," he told me. His eyes started to water, and he excused himself.

I checked my phone again, disappointed to see there still weren't any notifications. I was vaguely aware I wasn't just looking for a text from Jordan. I put the phone down, and scooped Hope out of her booster seat at the table. She squealed as I kissed her face all over. Even though I'd told her the night before that Viola was gone, she was too little to know what this meant. It made me sad to think Hope might not even remember her in a few years, especially since they'd been so close.

"Want to go play in the garden?" I asked.

"I help with flowers!" She tried to free herself from my arms, but I teased her by holding on tight. "Down Mama!"

"You can't walk on the floor, baby. It's hot lava!" She squealed as I flew her to the door. We spent a few hours digging in the dirt. I made progress on the weeds while Hope just made a mess. At lunchtime, I cleaned her up, and made us peanut butter and jelly sandwiches. I wanted to check my phone again, but kept it out of my reach. When it rang, though, I pounced on it, smiling when I read Jordan's name.

"Hey!"

"Hey yourself, babe," he said. "How are you feeling?"

"I'm all right. I didn't sleep all that well, and it's strange knowing she isn't here. But Hope and I have been distracting ourselves by working in the garden."

"If you're bored, you can come over here," he said.

"I can't," I told him. "I should stay here for Charlie. I don't know if he wants to go over any more arrangements. I think it's better if I'm available for him."

"Okay," Jordan said. "But if you change your mind, I'm free all day."

"Okay," I said, though I knew I wouldn't change my mind. Going to his house sounded better than being sad at home, but I couldn't leave Charlie alone, even if he stayed in his room for the rest of the day.

We only talked for a few minutes more before someone beeped in on his other line.

"Hey, this could be for work," he said. "I better go. I'll call you tomorrow, okay?"

I told him goodbye, and then turned back to Hope.

"Now what should we do?" I asked her. Her mouth was full of food, and she showed me what she was eating. "That's gross," I laughed.

After lunch, I took her for a walk past the vineyard and up into the hills—the same walk I'd taken with Jace. He was on my mind as the sound of birds and humming insects filled the space around us. *It's over*, I reminded myself. *You have Jordan now.*

We reached the ridge that looked down on the whole valley. Our house seemed so tiny from where I stood, the surrounding rows of vineyards appearing as patterned rectangles.

"Hello!" I shouted out, and grinned as my voice echoed through the trees. Hope giggled.

"Hey-yo!" she cried out, throwing her head back as she yelled. We took turns calling out to no one and everyone, and then listening for our voices to call back. When that got old, I carried her back down to the barn at the bottom of the trail. We peered inside, and I pointed out the large owl that slept in the rafters.

"Shhh," I whispered. "He's sleeping." I put my finger to my lips, and she copied me. Then I saw the giggle in her eyes.

"Hey-yo!" she cried out, and the giant bird flapped its wings, soaring over us and out of the barn. I turned and we watched as it flew out of view. Then we ventured inside and I turned over boards so we could watch the bugs and salamanders underneath try to escape. I picked up one small salamander and held it close to her. She was afraid to touch it, but studied it while it was in my hand. I released it, and we made our way back to the house.

That night, I was disappointed in my phone. By now, Jace would have texted another "reason" to me. I knew there wouldn't be any more, and part of me was glad. I didn't need his distractions to confuse me, but the other part of me would miss hearing from him, even if he was trying to hold on to something that never was.

I had Jordan now. He wasn't perfect, but he could be perfect for me. At least, he could be enough for me.

He had to be.

Good Together

"Can't you keep her quiet?" Charlie snapped. I closed my eyes for a moment and took a deep breath. Hope was crying on the carpet, upset that her block tower had fallen over again. She wanted to play on the hardwood, but I made her stop when she kept pushing it over. Charlie had complained about the noise, so my resolution was to have her work on the carpet, but the unsteady surface didn't allow her to build any towers; it kept falling without her help. Now she was throwing a tantrum.

"I'm trying," I said through clenched teeth. *He's grieving,* I reminded myself. For the past two days, he kept losing his patience. Remembering the last time he was like this, I'd done my best to keep my head while he lost his. But I was growing tired of taking the brunt of his mood.

"Well, try harder. I have a lot to do before the funeral tomorrow, and I can't think with all that racket." He left the room before I could respond, and I was glad. I wasn't sure how much longer I could keep from snapping back at him.

I looked outside and frowned at the rain that was keeping us inside. "Since when does it rain in June?" I muttered. I picked Hope up, but she pushed against me.

"No, Mama. Down!"

"How about we play in some puddles?" I asked. She immediately stopped crying, and her face lit up.

"I get my boots!" she said. She pushed against me again, and I set her down. She ran to the closet near the door and tried to pull the knob.

"Here, let me help you." I opened the door, and she lunged inside to grab her red boots. I slipped them on her feet, and then put on my own. Once our raincoats were on, we both went outside. Fátima was walking up the front steps with a tray of food.

"Hi! What are you doing here?" I asked. She wasn't supposed to work that day.

"I brought you some dinner for tonight."

"Please say it's tamales." We'd just eaten lunch, but my mouth watered at the thought of them. She lifted a corner of the foil. Once the steam cleared, I saw rows of wrapped tamales lying inside. "Thank you so much!"

"Where are you two going in this rain?" she asked.

"Well, Charlie is in one of his... I mean, we were a little too loud for him, so we're getting out of his hair and going to jump in some puddles."

"Fun for you, not for me," she said. "Muy sucio. Very dirty."

She went in the house, and Hope and I made our way slowly down the road as she stomped in every puddle we passed. I had to admit, it was cathartic to be in the rain, better than being cooped up in the house with Charlie as he sorted out his emotions. I couldn't hold it against him; this was foreign territory. He'd always been the rock of the household, standing strong when I was having a meltdown or Viola was frustrated because of her failing mind. When we fell apart, he remained our anchor. It was apparent how hard it was for him to be this fragile after her death. I wanted to be there for him in the same way he'd been for me, but didn't know how. For the past two days, he'd isolated himself except for the few times he'd snapped at Hope or me.

I was dealing with my own grief as well. Losing Viola was almost like losing one of my parents. I kept thinking of all the things I wished I'd said to her. Would she have understood? Viola chose me when everyone else rejected me. She rescued me from that parking lot. She saved my life. She saved Hope's life. I owed her everything.

The rain was coming down harder. While it wasn't cold, I figured it was time to make our way back inside where it was dry, but when I tried to take Hope's hand to lead her toward the house, she pulled away.

"No!" she insisted, stomping in a puddle for emphasis.

"Come on, baby. We can watch a movie and snuggle on the couch," I coaxed her. Truthfully, I didn't want to go inside either. I wanted to get out of the rain, but knew she'd be cranky and stir-crazy. I also knew Charlie needed his space.

"What do you say we get out of here?" I asked Hope. She was ignoring me, poking at a worm in the mud. "Want to go for a car ride?"

"See KK?" she asked. *Where did that come from?*

"No, baby." I'd been pushing Jace out of my head since we last spoke, though I also checked for texts from him regularly since Reason #2, trying not to be disappointed when there was nothing. I kept telling myself it was better this way. I didn't want him to fall for me. I was moving forward with Jordan. But, things were different with Jordan. While Jace was naturally attentive to me, Jordan was distant. To be fair, he'd always been this way. It was something I'd found appealing about him. He'd give me just enough attention to pull me in, then he'd back off so I was always reaching for him. It was a cat and mouse game I'd found infuriating and exhilarating. But now, I didn't have the energy for games, especially while trying to process my grief over Viola's death, and handle Charlie's temper and a bored toddler. I wanted Jordan to sense this, to call me just so he could hear me talk. But he wasn't good on the phone. Instead, he kept asking when I could come over to see him. I wanted to, but felt like this was the wrong time. Knowing Jordan, he'd want to fool around, and I wasn't in the mood. I needed someone to listen. I needed a friend. I needed someone who would hear what I had to say, keep quiet when I needed to talk, and tell me the words I needed to hear when I had nothing left to say. I needed someone to hold me because I needed to be held, and be there with me because he wanted to be near me.

I need Jace.

The thought hit me hard. No, I did *not* need Jace.

I pulled out my phone.

Me: *Are you free right now? Can we come over?*

The rain dotted the screen as I waited for a reply.

Jordan: *Come on over. :-)*

"Come on, Hope. Let's go to Jor… Let's go to Daddy's house." I took her hand, and she didn't argue. I didn't bother to go to the house, but led her to the garage and buckled her into her car seat.

She fell asleep on the way. I kept the music off as the rain hit the windshield, my thoughts moving back and forth in my head with the beat of the wipers. *Jace. Jordan. Jace. Jordan.* I hated that I was thinking like this. Jace was too young to take on the responsibility of a child. Hope was Jordan's responsibility. Jace was caring and sensitive. Jordan was unpredictable and lacked intuition. Jace would have to give up his whole life to be with me. Jordan looked at our daughter as if he wanted a future with us. Jace would make a good father.

"Jordan *is* Hope's father," I whispered.

Was this why I loved him, though? No. I loved him because he was home to me. He was everything familiar to me. He represented all I lost when I came to Petaluma. He was that part of me I wanted to keep. He was my youth, my innocence, my life before everything fell apart. He was my connection to the past as I moved into the future. Even after everything we'd been through, I couldn't let him go. He wanted to make it up to me. I *needed* him to make it up to me, and I *needed* him to make it up to Hope. I *needed* him so I could make peace with the past. Most of all, I *needed* him to love me in ways he couldn't when we were younger.

I *needed* a future with him.

I pulled up to Jordan's house, and peered at his door through the rain. Hope was still sleeping, and I dreaded waking her. The front door opened and Jordan ran out, barefoot like the last time, holding an umbrella. He opened the passenger door and leaned across to give me a kiss. His skin was warm against mine, and I inhaled his scent of tobacco and cologne. It was starting to grow on me. His lips lingered on mine, and then he pulled back and gave me a grin.

"I was starting to believe I'd never see you again," he said.

"It's only been two days," I reminded him.

"Longest two days of my life," he told me. The way he was looking at me made me feel warm inside. He peeked at the back seat, and I saw his face soften as he looked at

Hope. "Come out and hold the umbrella. I'll carry her in the car seat so she'll stay asleep."

I got out and trotted to the other side of the car. As I held the umbrella, he unbuckled her car seat. I closed the door and we went into the house.

The inside was as simple as the outside, though without weeds and peeling paint. Jordan led me through a narrow hallway to the living room, where there were plenty of places to sit. The room had a couch or chair for every corner, none of them matching, and all in well-loved condition, evidenced by a few threadbare patches. A throw rug took up the center of the room, covering a dark hardwood floor. There were a few posters on the walls, the kind you'd probably see in a teenage boy's bedroom—one was a girl in a bikini, another was of a sports car, and another was a black and white image of Marilyn Monroe. A stale scent of cigarettes lingered in the air, and I wrinkled my nose as I glanced at the filled ashtray on the table.

"Ever think about quitting?" I asked as he set Hope down. He looked at me, and then at the ashtray.

"Sorry," he said, picking it up and emptying it in the trash. "Since you guys are going to be over here more, the roommates and I will start smoking outside." He pulled me down on the couch. Even as I stifled a laugh to keep from waking Hope, I felt strange at how relaxed he was with me, holding me like no time had passed between us. For a moment, I recalled how much it hurt when he drove away, and how I ached when he didn't come back. I brushed that aside and smiled up at him. He kissed the tip of my nose.

"Want to watch a movie?" he asked. I didn't. I wanted to talk, to get past what happened and move on, to talk about how sad I was now that Viola was gone, and how I wished I could help Charlie with his grief. I wanted to share how hard it was to trust him, and yet trusting him was all I longed to do. I wanted to tell him how angry I was at him for so long, how happy I was to be here with him now, how scared I was about the future, and how excited I was now that we could be a family. I wanted to reveal my fears, and have him take them away.

But I didn't know how to say any of that.

"Sure," I said. He got up and took out a few movie. We settled on *Gladiator*, and I curled up under his arm as the familiar music started. I'd seen it a few times, but liked it enough that I didn't mind watching it again. Jordan seemed to have different ideas, though. The movie had only been playing for fifteen minutes when he leaned over to kiss my mouth. I let him, but pulled back when the kiss got more intense.

"What's wrong?" he asked.

"Well, for one, Hope is right there."

"She's sleeping."

"Well, your roommates might come home at any minute."

"They're at a basketball game and won't be back until late."

"Then…"

"I'm not going anywhere, Maddie," he told me.

"It's not that," I said. "It's just…" I tried to figure out what exactly I was feeling.

"It's just *what*?"

"It's just, I'm not sure if I'm ready for this."

"Ready for what?"

"This. Us. Acting like we're in some sort of relationship." I pulled away and sat at the corner of the couch. He gave me a confused look.

"I don't understand. We've known each other for years. We've been together for years."

"Wrong, we've been apart since the day you left three years ago."

"I tried to explain that to you! I messed up. I'm sorry. I want to make it up to you; I'm trying to make it up to you. But I don't know what you want me to do."

"I want… I want you to take it slow with me. Don't be so familiar. I want you to date me, not be in a relationship with me."

"So, you want to see other people," he said. His eyes darkened, and I reached over and touched his hand.

"No, I don't want to see anyone else, and I don't want you to, either. I want us to end up together, and I want that to be our main goal. But to get there, I need to get to know you better, and I need you to get to know me."

"I already know you."

I shook my head.

"No, you don't. And I don't know you, either. We're different people than we were back when we were together. We've changed. I want to get to know the person you are now, and I want you to see who I am, as well."

"I see you, Maddie," he said. He took my hand and shifted closer. He pressed his forehead to mine, and placed his other hand behind the back of my neck. He stayed there for a moment, and we breathed. When he pulled away, I looked into his face. He was still there, the Jordan I fell in love with. But in just three years, I saw the changes in him, too. There was a new kind of calm, even under his rough exterior. I wondered if he'd figured life out yet. The old Jordan seemed unreachable, and I'd sometimes felt like a temporary part of his life. But this Jordan appeared ready to commit to me and be a father to Hope. At least, this was what I longed for. Was this really him, or was it what I wanted him to be?

"I see you, and I hear you," he told me. "We'll take it slow. Today we'll watch a movie and just hang out. Tomorrow, maybe we can go to the zoo or something."

"Tomorrow is Viola's funeral," I told him. He looked confused for a second, and then a look of clarity crossed his face.

"Oh, that lady you're living with." I winced at the way he described her, as if she was a roommate instead of family.

"She was more than just some lady I lived with," I told him, pulling away.

"Hey," he said. "I'm sorry. I didn't know. You're right, I need to get to know you better, including the parts of your life I know nothing about. But you need to give me a chance. If I'm acting insensitive, it's not on purpose. Educate me, don't pull away."

I nodded. He brought me back toward him, though I folded myself up in his arms. He rested his head on mine, and then kissed the top of it. "Don't shut me out," he murmured.

"I'm not trying to," I said, even as I stayed bent in a weird pretzel shape against his body. He poked at my side, and I twitched involuntarily, and couldn't help smiling. He took that moment to steal a kiss, and I only hesitated for a second. When his tongue touched my lips, I opened them, letting him in and lowering my guard. His hands stayed at my shoulders, but his mouth revealed his true desire as he reminded me why I'd fallen in love with him. He let go of my mouth and lowered his face into my hair.

"We're good together, aren't we?" he whispered, his lips brushing my ear. I shivered, his touch sent a shock through my body.

"When we're not making babies," I whispered back, and he leaned away from me to shoot me a grin.

"I don't know, I think we did pretty good at that, too." He glanced over at Hope at the same time I did. When I looked back at him, he was giving me a look I'd seen too many times. I shook my head.

"Jordan," I warned him, though I felt myself bending under his gaze. I wasn't sure I was strong enough to hold on to my principles.

"Maddie," he whispered. "I'll be gentle. I want to show you how much I've missed you. Let me make love to you."

His words pierced me. I closed my eyes, trying to find my evaporating resolve. The Jordan I knew did not make love. He was intense, and he took control. He left me wanting more. He satisfied the primal urges inside me. But he did not make love. I opened my eyes and looked at him.

"You don't know how to make love," I told him. I wanted to move, but I couldn't. His eyes had me pinned.

"Let me show you," he whispered. I glanced down at Hope. She was still asleep, and probably would be for a while. He took my chin and turned it back toward him. "It's just us, right now. You and me, like old times. But this time, I want to show you how much I've missed you, and how much I love you." I started to close my eyes, but he reached over and touched my cheek until I was looking at him again. "Don't close your eyes."

He carried me to his room, but left the door open upon my insistence so I could hear Hope if she woke up. Then he pulled my clothes off my body, piece by piece, slowly, taking his time, admiring each part of me he exposed. He saved my bra and panties for last, leaving them on as he kissed my neck, my shoulders, down my arm to my wrists. My hand lingered against the stubble on his cheek, and he rubbed it against the my forearm until I had goosebumps from the tingling. His eyes locked with mine as he reached around my back. I gasped when my bra fell away. He sucked in a breath of air.

"You are so beautiful," he whispered, his blue eyes finding mine again. He captured my mouth, pressing his clothed body against my near naked one. He trailed his kisses down my body, his tongue teasing every part of me as he inched closer to my underwear. I was watching him, my breath shallow as I waited to see what he would do next. He lifted his head, a wicked glint in his eyes. Then my underwear was off and I was lying in front of him naked on his bed. His gaze found my tattoo. He kissed that area first. I held my breath as he continued kissing me, inching closer to my most sensitive part until he was there and I couldn't keep my eyes open any longer. I let him take me with his mouth, the warm waves of ecstasy washing over me until I couldn't contain myself. I buried my face in one of the pillows as I cried out, keeping my voice muffled as he brought me to completion. When I was done, he stripped his clothes off and lowered his body to mine.

"Condom," I breathed.

"Maddie." I couldn't open my eyes. I was so lost in this moment. But I'd be damned if I got pregnant again.

"Condom," I insisted. He laughed, and got up. I opened my eyes and watched as he tore one from a package and slipped it on. I'd forgotten how beautiful his body was. His sculpted chest had more tattoos than before, but he was bare from his stomach to his thighs. When he came closer,

I moved my hand to the place where his belly formed a V. Then I cupped him and guided him to me. He fell against me, and then he filled me. I gasped against his chest, doing my best to keep quiet. He turned my face so that I watched him, and then moved slowly inside of me. I wanted to look away, but he wouldn't let me. Every time I closed my eyes, he stopped. When I opened them, he continued. His need for control was both frustrating and irresistible. He kept it slow, and I clutched at him as the anticipation built. All the while, his eyes held mine. I felt dizzy from his touch, his scent, the intensity of his gaze. He grabbed hold of my mouth as he pushed hard against me, and I gasped as my body responded. His rhythm quickened and I felt the pressure inside me mounting. Soon I was exploding, biting my lip to keep from making any sounds. I wanted to scream. I wanted to let loose. It took everything I had to keep from crying out.

He finished, and then lowered his body on mine. I clutched at him, unwilling to let him go. He stayed where he was as I wrapped my legs and arms around him, holding him as tight as I could while I recovered. His skin was sweaty, and I kissed the salty moisture from his shoulder. He pulled me even tighter, and we remained that way until we heard Hope cry in the next room.

I got up to put on my clothes, but paused to take in the length of his naked body across his bed.

"You better get dressed, too." He groaned and buried his head in his pillow.

"Woman, you've taken all my energy. Can't I just stay here and sleep?" I responded by throwing his shirt at him.

We spent the rest of the afternoon with him. He didn't have any toys there, but Hope seemed content to watch cartoons between us on the couch while the rain fell outside. It felt right, like we'd always been a family. While she watched the show, Jordan told me about the friends he'd met since moving to San Rafael, and about his buddy who got him into tattooing. I told him about my life at our vineyard house, and about Charlie and Viola. He wiped away my tears as I reminisced about the way Viola used to play with Hope, and how much I missed her.

"It's going to be okay," he told me. "At least she's not hurting anymore."

Just before dinnertime, he walked me to my car, buckling Hope's car seat and strapping her in. When the door closed, he hugged me.

"When can I see you again?" he asked. I thought about what I could expect from the next day. Charlie had been so distant. Fátima was helping with the food. I'd be on my own with Hope. I didn't want to be alone.

"Come with me tomorrow," I said. As soon as I said it, all the things that could go wrong began racing through my head.

"Are you sure?" he asked.

Charlie would hate this. But he was going to be so preoccupied with guests he wouldn't even notice. It would be fine. I needed someone there for me. I was hurting, too. Jordan had changed....

"Yes," I said. "Meet me at St. Andrew's in Petaluma." He punched the address into his phone, and then kissed me goodbye. My doubts about inviting him to the funeral faded as he reminded me what I had to look forward to for the rest of my life.

"I'll miss you until then," he said.

Saying Goodbye

What did I do?

I woke up realizing I was about to introduce Jordan as my boyfriend at Viola's funeral. It was a selfish decision. I knew I needed to come clean to Charlie, especially since I knew this thing with Jordan wasn't a fling, but something real. But not today. Not when we were saying goodbye to Charlie's wife.

"How could I be so stupid?" I muttered, picking up my phone. There was already a text from Jordan staring back at me.

Jordan: *Should I wear a suit today?*

I wasn't sure how to respond. Did I go through with this and hope for the best? Or did I tell him not to come? In the end, I followed my head.

Me: *About that, I think this might not be such a good idea.*

I waited for his answer, but none came. I was about to give up and get dressed when my phone rang.

"What are you talking about?" Jordan asked when I answered.

"I just… Charlie's not going to be in a good space today. He's lost his wife. I don't want to tell him I'm dating you on the day of Viola's funeral."

"You haven't told him about us?"

I paused. I hadn't quite mentioned that to Jordan yet.

"I didn't know how," I said. "I wasn't sure how he'd take it. He's spent the last couple of years taking care of Hope and me after…well… you know. And he's been the one paying for Hope's and my needs. He's even paying for my college."

"So this is about money," Jordan spat. "If you wanted child support, why didn't you tell me instead of just using me?"

"Excuse me?"

"Tell me how much I owe so I can be your boyfriend, and I'll write him a check," he demanded.

"It's not about money!" I yelled. "It's just that he might not have a good impression of you. That's all."

"Because you've been trashing me over the past three years."

"No!" I insisted. "Well, not exactly. I mean, I haven't been trashing you, but I was pretty hurt. I didn't know why you left me, and why you never came back."

"I told you why! By the time I got out, I didn't know where to find you!"

"But I didn't know that then!" I told him. "All I knew was that I was left alone to raise our daughter without any help from you. I tried to get over it, but it wasn't easy."

He was silent for a moment, but I could hear him breathing.

"It's a good thing I found you when I did. Then you couldn't poison our daughter against me, too." I heard the click, and the line went dead.

I stared at the phone, not sure what to do. Call him back? Apologize?

"No," I told myself as I tossed the phone on the bed. It pinged again. I tried to ignore it, but I gave in.

Jace: *Reason #3: You forgive those who have wronged you, even if other people don't understand.*

"You have no idea," I told the phone. Part of me wished Jace would just keep his promise of never speaking to me again. But seeing his name brought a sense of comfort. For a moment, I longed for the time before I told him goodbye, when things seemed simpler. I thought I was sure about what I wanted. Now, I didn't know what that was.

"A life with Jordan," I whispered. I knew we'd make things right before the day was through. But not now. Right now, I needed to focus on getting ready for Viola's funeral and being there for Charlie, even if he pushed me away.

I turned my phone on airplane mode to keep away distractions, then hid it in my dresser. I peeked in on Hope, who was quietly playing in her crib. When she saw me in her doorway, she stood up and held out her arms.

"Up, Mama!" she cried, reaching over the rail. I picked her up, and she squealed as I pulled her in for a spinning hug. Then we went back to my room so I could take a quick bath while she played. Once I was dressed, we headed to the kitchen. Charlie was sitting at the counter with a cup of coffee. He set it down as I put Hope in her booster seat.

"Did you sleep well?" he asked. I nodded. There was an obvious tension in the room, and I tried to bat it away.

"I did. Did you?"

"Surprisingly, yes. I didn't think I would, especially since today is…" He trailed off, his eyes watering. I put my arms around him. "Can you forgive this old man?" he asked. I kissed him on the cheek.

"What am I supposed to forgive? You've done nothing wrong."

"I've been a grouch."

"You're mourning your wife. You're allowed. Besides, you're doing way better than I would if it were me. I only knew Viola three years. You've loved her for a lifetime. It's going to take some getting used to."

Charlie wrapped his arms around me and returned my hug. It felt like a lifetime ago when he'd held me like this for the first time, a time when I was grieving my own loss—the day I gave birth to Hope, and then gave her away. I'd had nothing, and no one. Once Hope left my arms, there was nothing left. This realization hit me as I'd started to walk back toward the Winstons' house from the fire station where I left Hope. I didn't even have a home.

Charlie had found me crumpled in his driveway.

"I couldn't keep her," I'd told him, unable to say anything else. He didn't ask any questions. He just picked me up as if I were a child, and carried me to his car, taking me back to the place I'd soon call home.

Now in his kitchen, we embraced over our mutual sadness. This house wouldn't be the same without Viola.

"You're a special girl," he said. "Thank you for being part of our family. I don't know what I would do today if you weren't here with me."

"Thank you." I kissed him again, and began to make us all breakfast.

***

Charlie and I sat in the front row of St. Andrew's with a few distant relatives I hadn't met, and more than a hundred friends and business acquaintances in the wooden pews behind us.

The priest stood before the congregation next to a table that held the largest bouquet of flowers I'd ever seen, a photo of Viola, and the urn holding her ashes. Charlie had decided we'd sprinkle them over the soil in the vineyard, allowing her to be a part of the growth cycle of the wine we were producing. The rest would be scattered at sea.

Father Sebastian's voice rang through the church, the sound echoing off the walls so that it seemed like a song. He began by sharing about Viola's life, even though I was pretty sure he didn't know her. In all the time I'd lived with the Winstons, we'd never gone to church. I knew they had a religious background, though. Perhaps they went here before.

My mind wandered as the priest continued. A statue of Mary was stationed near the front corner of the church, seeming to project peace with the gentle expression on her face. But I couldn't stop looking at the stain glass windows surrounding the top portion of the church's tall walls, showing the scene leading to Jesus' crucifixion. It scared me. It was also beautiful.

I inhaled the scent of incense in the air, comparing it to the lavender-vanilla scent in Hope's hair as she sat in my lap. Both were comforting, though only one was familiar.

Father Sebastian finished talking, then invited Charlie and me to the front. I handed Hope to Fátima sitting next to me, and followed Charlie to the pulpit. Charlie went first, telling how he met Viola. As he spoke, I saw a familiar face in the last row. Jordan looked back at me. *Why is he here?* I glanced at Charlie, wondering if he noticed the stranger among his friends and family, but he seemed not to notice, sharing about their early years and how happy she was when their daughter, Ellie, was born.

"When Ellie died," Charlie began, then paused, choking back a sob. I took his hand.

"Go on," I whispered. "I've got you." He squeezed my hand and faced forward. I did, too, but I only saw one person.

Sorry, Jordan mouthed. I didn't know what to do. He shouldn't have been there.

"When Ellie died," Charlie repeated, "I thought I'd lose Viola, too. She was meant to be a mother. Even though we'd lost Ellie long before she was gone, her death rocked us. We never fully recovered. I disappeared into my work; Viola disappeared into her mind. For those of you who know us well, the past several decades were really hard as we tried to move beyond Ellie's death." Charlie squeezed my hand again as he turned toward me. "It wasn't until this girl came along that the light came back into our house." I felt warm knowing everyone was looking at me, but I focused on Charlie. "Maddie, you and Hope have brought such joy to Viola and me. You've brought youth and laughter into our lives, and you're very much like a daughter to us. You made Viola's life so happy in these last three years. She adored you and Hope."

"We loved her, too," I said as I hugged him. He continued talking about Viola, and ended by thanking everyone for coming to say goodbye to her. Then he motioned for me to take the microphone. I felt shy as I moved forward, especially since I already knew what I wanted to say.

"I was homeless before I met Viola and Charlie," I said, beginning my story of living on the street, when I was unsure where I would find my next meal and aware I couldn't provide for my unborn child.

"Viola picked me," I said. "I hoped to find work, and she was the one who saw me first. She and Charlie took me into their home, fed me, cared for me, and gave me work so I could afford food. I hid my homelessness from them, but they saw through my lies. When Hope was born, they invited us to live with them." I avoided Jordan's face as I spoke, looking everywhere but at him. "If it weren't for them, I would have died. At the very least, I wouldn't have been able to keep my daughter. I was in no place to raise a child. My parents had rejected me. I was on my own. I could hardly take care of myself." I accidentally glanced at Jordan, and quickly looked away, but not before I saw the graveness in his expression. I turned to Charlie, and the warmth in his face comforted me. "Viola and Charlie gave me chance to be a mother. They loved us as if we were their own. It doesn't matter that we don't share the same blood. We're family." I felt the tears in my eyes as I smiled at Charlie. "Viola was my mother. I wasn't born to her, but it doesn't matter. She's my mother, and I'm her daughter. I'm going to miss her with everything I am."

I ended it there, tears streaming down my cheeks. I scanned the back pew, and saw an empty space where Jordan had been sitting. I was relieved, yet disappointed to see him gone.

The funeral ended with the priest waving incense from a metal censer, walking down the aisle with us following. Charlie held the urn in one arm, and I held his other. We stood at the back of the church as family and friends came out, offering condolences before heading to our house for the wake.

"I go take care of food and greet people," Fátima said, handing me Hope. She kissed me on the cheek.. "You were lovely," she said. "Both of you."

After twenty minutes, only a few people remained in the church. I started toward the car so I could put Hope in her car seat.

"Mr. Winston," I heard. My heart thumped loudly as I turned around and saw Jordan coming up to Charlie. He was wearing a suit and a tie, something I never thought I'd see him in. He had an earnest expression on his face, and I felt guilty to wish him away. He held his hand out, and I wanted to disappear as Charlie took it.

"Did you know Viola?" he asked.

"I didn't," Jordan said. "But I know Maddie. I'm Jordan Turner."

"Jordan," Charlie repeated. I saw recognition slowly cross his face. His friendly smile evaporated, replaced by a stern expression. He looked at me.

"I can explain," I said. He turned back to Jordan.

"I'm sure you have some kind of reason for being here today, or even why you've been missing for the past three years," Charlie said. "Hell, I bet there's even a reason why Maddie has chosen to accept you back into her life after all you've put her through. But today, I don't want to hear it."

"Mr. Winston," Jordan began, but Charlie silenced him with a shake of his head.

"If you'll excuse me, I have a house full of people who want to help me say goodbye to my wife." He brushed past Jordan and headed down the walkway. "Maddie, it's time to go."

I turned to Jordan. I opened my mouth, but his expression silenced me. I saw the anger in his face, but he still gave me a small smile.

"I'll call you tonight," he said. Then he headed down the path that led to the parking lot behind the church.

Charlie didn't speak to me during the ride. By the time we arrived home, he'd masked his anger with a warm smile, and he greeted each guest as if the exchange between Jordan and him never happened. This was scarier than if he'd come unglued on me. I hung in the background, helping Fátima in the kitchen and making sure Hope stayed out of trouble. I masqueraded as a server rather than a grieving family member. Not everyone went along with my plan to keep from socializing, though. Several times, I was forced into small talk, and I went along with it even though I felt like crawling in bed and forgetting all about this day. I wished everyone would leave, though I also dreaded it because then I'd have to face Charlie. I was filled with anxiety by the time people began going home. I put Hope to bed when only a few guests remained. After the last person was gone, I helped Fátima with the cleanup. I didn't want her to leave, knowing Charlie was waiting until the house was empty before we talked. But once I kissed her goodbye, I knew it was time.

I knocked at Charlie's study door as soon as she was gone.

"Come in." He was leaning back in his chair, waiting as I sat down. Then he closed his eyes and sighed.

"I'm sorry. I ran into him a few days ago. I was mad; I wanted to hate him. But he's changed. He's sorry he left. We were both so young. He was scared. By the time he realized, it was too late."

"What happened to that other boy?" Charlie asked.

"Jace and I didn't work out."

"But that was just last week. I thought you were serious about him."

"I was. It's just…it's complicated. It doesn't matter anyway. I ran into Jordan after breaking up with Jace. I want to make things work with him. He's grown up in the past three years, and he loves Hope so much. She loves him, too."

"But do you love him?" he asked me.

"I think so," I said.

"You *think* so?"

"No, I mean, I *do* love him. It's…well, it's different." Charlie's expression softened and I relaxed, opening up about my unresolved anger and fears. "I want to give Jordan a chance," I said. "I want Hope to know her father. And…" I paused, glancing away. "And I'm sorry that I didn't tell you before. I'm sorry that you had to find out today, especially in that way."

He didn't say anything for a while. We both stared at his desk in uncomfortable silence. Finally, he cleared his throat. I looked at him, and he gave a smile as his peace offering. I breathed in deeply, the load on my shoulders falling away.

"Well, I'm not sure any day would have been a great day to learn about this, but it doesn't have to be all bad. If you think you're making the right decision, I'll support you. But I want to get to know him, first. After all, if he's going to be dating my daughter and caring for my granddaughter, he should probably have a chance to suck up to me. Invite him over for dinner tomorrow night. Let's start over."

I bounced from my chair and threw myself at Charlie.

"Thank you so much." I could still hear his warm laugh as I ran from the room so I could grab my phone and call him.

The phone was still on airplane mode. I turned my data back on and waited for my phone to catch up. After thirty seconds, it started to ping. One message. Two messages. Eight messages and a voicemail.

Seven of the texts were Jordan apologizing, trying to get through to me, and finally saying he was going to show up so he could apologize in person. I paused at the eighth one.

Jace: *Reason #4. You still read my texts. I know, because your iPhone tells on you.*

I grinned at the way he called me out. I hit the voicemail button, and then listened as Jace's voice hit my ear.

"Hey Maddie. I saw in the newspaper that Viola's funeral was today. I know today will be hard for you, so I thought I'd break our silent treatment to let you know I'm here if you need to talk. I mean, I know you have a boyfriend you can talk with, but… I probably shouldn't have called you since you have a boyfriend. Actually, I *know* I shouldn't call you. I guess… I guess I just want you to know we can still be friends. I don't mean the 'let's be friends' line two people say when they'll never speak to each other again. I mean the 'let's be genuine friends and stay in each other's life.' Thing is, I kind of like you as a person, and I'd like to hang out with you even if I can't kiss you… God, that sounds stupid. What I mean is, Kayci misses her buddy and she wants to hang out again. So if you can't do it for me, would you do it for KK? You wouldn't let down a three-year-old, would you? I didn't think so. Call me back and let's pick a date."

I looked at my phone, shaking my head. "Jace," I said with a small laugh. I wanted to call him, but I knew I needed to talk with Jordan first. I dialed Jordan's number, but it went to voicemail. After the prompt, I said, "Hey, I have something big to ask you, so call me as soon as you get this."

Since he wasn't picking up, I called Jace back. He picked up after the fourth ring.

"Hey," he said. It sounded like he'd been running.

"Are you working out or something?"

"Or something," he said. "I wasn't in the room when you called and ran to pick up before it went to voicemail." Then he groaned. "God, I'm so smooth. I probably shouldn't have admitted that. In fact, I should have just let it go to voicemail. Can you call back so I can ignore you and then you'll think I'm cool?"

"It's too late," I told him. "I can see you nerd flag from here."

"Dang it. I was hoping I had that tucked away."

"It's all right. I sometimes color-coordinate my socks to match my own nerd flag."

"A nerd after my own heart," he said.

There was a pause, and I knew he felt as awkward as I did.

"So, KK wants us to hang out, huh?" I said, breaking the silence.

"Oh, yeah! She practically tore my arm off, trying to get me to call you. In fact, she was kind of disappointed when you didn't answer your phone. I had to tell her you were doing something very important." He stopped talking, and I heard him sigh. "Are you okay?" he asked, his tone serious. I closed my eyes. Today had been long and sad, but not terrible. It was a sweet farewell worthy of a woman like Viola.

"I've had better, but the funeral was nice, and a lot of people showed up, even…" I stopped myself before I said Jordan's name.

"Even *who*?"

I wasn't sure how to answer. *Hell, he wants to be friends? Let's see what he can handle.* "Even Jordan," I said. He was silent, and I was sure he'd eventually hang up on me.

"So, Charlie knows you two are dating?" This conversation was a mistake.

"Um, no," I admitted. "Well, he didn't. Now he does."

"How did he take it?"

"As expected. I told Jordan not to come, but he came anyway. When he introduced himself, Charlie was shocked. Then he was angry. But tonight after everyone left, he surprised me by being supportive. He even wants Jordan to come over for dinner tomorrow."

"Oh." Again, the line went quiet. I waited it out to see if he had anything else to say. He did. "Maybe this was a mistake."

Instantly, I felt bad. I didn't want to hurt him. I didn't even want him out of my life. I missed being around him, and I missed Kayci. I realized I even enjoyed reading his texts, knowing he was thinking of me. I wanted a life with Jordan. I also wanted Jace in my life. Was it possible to have both?

"It's not a mistake," I told him. "Don't hang up."

"I'm not."

"Maybe there needs to be rules to this friendship."

"Like, I can't talk about all the girls I'm messing around with." I wrinkled my nose at the thought, realizing I didn't want to hear about that any more than he wanted to hear about Jordan.

"Exactly," I told him. "And I won't talk about any guys I'm messing around with."

"Perfect," he said. "Then I guess we can be friends."

"Great, friend. Now, when are we going to hang out and let the girls play together?" I asked.

"Is tomorrow too soon?"

I thought about dinner with Charlie and Jordan that night. Would it be weird to see Jace before? *No, we're just friends. There's nothing wrong with this.*

"Tomorrow would be perfect. Let's meet at noon so they can play before Hope's nap."

The phone beeped, and I pulled it from my ear to see who was calling. *Jordan.*

"Hey, I need to go. It's… Uh, I just need to go." I could practically hear him roll his eyes as he gave a light laugh.

"Yeah, okay, friend. I'll see you tomorrow."

I switched over.

"Hey," I said.

"Hey. Were you on the other line?" Jordan asked.

"No." *Why did I just lie?*

"Weird. It sounded like you clicked over."

"That's strange. Guess what?"

"You tell me."

"Charlie wants you to come over tomorrow night for dinner. He wants to start over. He said he's going to be supportive since he knows how important this is."

"That's great," Jordan said. He didn't sound enthusiastic, though.

"What's wrong?"

"Nothing. It's just… Don't you think it's weird that he's fine with this?"

"No, not really. I think it's great." I didn't know what he was getting at. Charlie was giving us the green light, and Jordan was throwing up flags. "We caught Charlie off guard when you showed up at the funeral. Plus, this has been a really hard time for him. I think he realizes this is a good thing, that he should get to know you instead of making a snap judgment."

"You mean a judgment based on what you told him about me."

I stopped, trying to find the right words.

"I'm sorry," he said. "I'm not mad. I understand why you told him the things you did. You didn't know what was going on with me. You were in a hard position. You needed someone to be mad at."

Even as he apologized, his words made me angry. I needed someone to be mad at? I wasn't aware of what *he* was going through?

"Do you have any idea what *I* was going through?" I asked him.

"Babe, I'm not trying to minimize what happened to you. I already told you how bad I feel that I couldn't be there for you. But how could I? It's not like I could ask the warden to let me out of jail so I could look for my girl and our kid."

"I know. I'm sorry. This is all weird and wonderful and scary. Just be patient with me, okay?"

"Only if you're patient with me, too. It's new for both of us, but we're going to make it work. Believe me?"

"I believe you."

"Good," he said. "Now, tell me about this dinner Charlie has planned."

"There's not much to tell. He just wants to get to know you better."

"I guess I better be on my best behavior, right? But afterwards, we should go park the car and mess around."

"Jordan! I never should have given in to you."

"Babe, I can't think of anything else since yesterday. How about you? Have you thought of me?"

I blushed, recalling the times today, even in the middle of everything, when I shivered at the memory of his touch.

"Not once," I said.

"Really, so you don't remember when I—"

"I remember!" My cheeks were on fire as I thought of him undressing me, kissing me, looking at me, filling me...

"That's only the beginning," he promised.

It's Complicated

It was a perfect day for the park. There were only a few clouds in the sky, and the wind was minimal at best. I carried Hope as I walked along the pathway toward the playground, scanning the dozens of families who were also playing around the park.

Hope saw Kayci first when I reached the sand. She wiggled in my arms, pointing toward her. Jace stood from a squatting position and shot me a warm grin.

I set Hope down, and she quickly abandoned me.

"KK!" she cried, running to her friend. Kayci turned around and squealed at the sight of Hope, and then pulled her over to the sand toys.

"I guess they don't need time to warm up to each other," Jace said, coming over to me. He moved to give me a hug. I inhaled his citrus scent, and the smell went straight to my heart. When he pulled away, I realized again how handsome he was. I tried not to stare, but I couldn't help it: his unshaven face, his golden brown eyes, the way he was looking back at me… I cleared my throat. *You broke up with him, remember?*

"How've you been?" I asked him. He rolled his eyes.

"Oh, you know, just nursing some wounds."

"Jace."

"I'm fine," he insisted. "I've been working a lot, and hanging out with Kayci. How about you?"

"Same as yesterday. Fine as can be expected." Today, Charlie seemed back to his old self. There was still a sadness around him, but there also seemed to be a sense of relief. I supposed he could finally move forward now that the funeral was over. "It's going to be strange not having Viola there. I keep thinking she'll be in her room."

"Has Hope noticed yet?"

"A couple times she tried to open Viola's door. Other than that, not really. I think she's too young to understand."

We stopped talking and watched the girls play together. Kayci was digging a hole and Hope was slowly filling it again.

"Kayci, watch where you're flinging sand," Jace said. She paused, looked behind her, and then continued to dig. "Excuse me for a second." He got up and knelt down next to her, helping to dig the hole. As he did, he showed her how to scoop so sand didn't fly everywhere. Then he turned to Hope and showed her how to make hills with the sand. The girls liked the attention. I watched the way Hope tried to do everything he was doing.

I thought back to the day I broke things off, telling him he wasn't ready to have a relationship with someone like me. In truth, I was the one who wasn't ready. Seeing him now, I knew I was wrong: he would have been wonderful to Hope. He *was* wonderful to Hope. Why hadn't I seen this before?

"What?" he asked. I realized I was staring. I looked away as he came over. He sat next to me and nudged my shoulder. "What are you thinking?"

"Nothing," I said quickly.

"Too bad you can't have me, huh?" he said, winking. I nudged his shoulder back, and he took my hand in his. I looked down at the way our fingers fit together.

"Tell me to stop if you don't like it," he said. My heart pounded. I turned toward him, and couldn't look away.

"Friends hold hands sometimes," I whispered. He was staring at my mouth as I said it, and I caught my breath. This was wrong. I knew I shouldn't be here with him. What would Jordan think if he were here?

I turned away, but I didn't let go of his hand.

"Tell me why," Jace said.

"Why what?"

"Why he's better than me."

I closed my eyes. Still, I kept hold of his hand.

"Jace, don't do this."

He took my chin and turned my face to him.

"I need to know. Why do you love him? What does he have that I don't?"

It hurt to look at him. Everything that made me sure I was supposed to be with Jordan was starting to disappear.

"He's Hope's father."

"That's not enough."

"Isn't it, though?" I asked. "We made a child together. Now he wants to be a part of our lives."

"But do you love him?"

"We have a history together."

"Do you love him?"

He squeezed my hand, and I focused on our clasped fingers. If I loved Jordan, would I be holding another boy's hand? I pulled my hand away.

"Yes," I told him.

"I don't believe you."

I glared at him. "How can you even say that? You don't know me. You don't know him. You don't know what we've been through."

"No, but I know how much he hurt you."

I wrapped my arms around my knees and pulled them in tight, keeping my eyes on the girls so I wouldn't cry.

"It's complicated, okay," I said, then sighed. "We promised we wouldn't do this," I reminded him. "Remember? We're not supposed to talk about each other's love lives." I watched as he played with the sand in front of him.

"I know." He shook his head. "I'm sorry. This is selfish. I want to be with you. I care about you. I don't want to see you with anyone but me. But this is also about not wanting to see you hurt. I can't help but feel this is going to end badly, for you and for Hope."

I wanted to argue, but it wasn't anything I hadn't thought about already. I'd let so much of my guard down; if Jordan disappointed me, I didn't know how I'd recover.

"I need to give him a chance," I said. He closed his eyes and sighed. When he opened them again, he gave me a small smile.

"We would have been great together, you know," he told me.

"That's not fair."

"Tell me I'm lying."

"I can't."

He took my hand again. Then he pulled me close and put his arm around me. I leaned my head on his shoulder, pretending things weren't the way they were. For a moment, I was just Maddie, and he was just Jace.

"If you could have anything you wanted, what would it be?" Jace asked. I didn't answer right away. I wasn't even sure. My whole life, I'd gone along for the ride. From the moment I got pregnant to bring taken in by the Winstons, everything had been decided for me. Even now, preparing for a career in the winery business and a future with Jordan, it felt like a whirlwind—and I was trying to catch my breath.

None of this had been my decision. Not one move I made was something I chose. I'd had my whole life chosen for me. I was free…but was I really? Did I really want this life?

"I don't want anything," I told Jace, turning toward him. "I have everything I need."

"Liar," he said, but his eyes held his smile. I didn't disagree with him. I also didn't answer. I wouldn't have known how.

We let the girls stay a little longer. We took them to feed the ducks, then walked them around the perimeter of the park before saying goodbye.

"I'll see you soon." Jace hugged me goodbye. We lingered for a moment. My face was close to his while I was still in his embrace. Why did he have to make this so hard? I pulled away first, and he let me go.

"Goodbye."

Just a Game

"Let's use the nice dishes, don't you think?" Charlie asked, stirring the spaghetti sauce. I gave him a look.

"They're all nice dishes. Do you mean the flowered ones we only use on holidays?"

"Those would be the ones," he said with a wink. I pulled them down and gave them a quick rinse in the sink. Once they were dry, I set them on the table. Hope was already in her booster seat with a few crackers in front of her to keep her occupied. She played happily with her food, but I was a nervous wreck. This dinner meant so much to me. I wanted Charlie to like Jordan, but I recognized that was a tall order. He didn't know much about Jordan at all, and what he did know wasn't good—Jordan took off after I was caught lifting that woman's wallet, it was his idea for me to lift it in the first place, and he never came back for me. Charlie didn't know Jordan's history with petty theft, or that he spent time in jail, but he didn't need to know any of that to dislike Jordan. Charlie had taken care of Hope and me, taking the place of father and caregiver while Jordan was out of the picture. Knowing Charlie, this was one dark mark against Jordan that he'd have trouble redeeming. And knowing how charming Jordan could be, he still had a chance of turning things around.

As I set the last glass on the table, the doorbell rang. I smoothed my shirt, even though Jordan didn't care much about appearance, and I went to the door.

"Hey," he said, giving me a light kiss at the corner of my mouth. I grinned when I saw how nervous he was. "Shut up," he whispered with a smirk.

"You look nice," I said. He wore a button-up plaid shirt, a pair of dark khakis, and loafers. Just the tip of the tattoo near his neck was showing. He almost looked clean-cut. Almost. "You should dress like that more often," I teased him. He opened his mouth to say something to me, but stopped, his attention diverted to just behind me.

"Mr. Winston," he said, extending his hand. I moved out of the way so they could have a proper handshake.

"I hope you brought your appetite. I made enough spaghetti to feed a small crowd."

"Smells delicious, sir." We made our way to the table where Charlie had placed a large bowl of pasta. I cut up some for Hope and put it in front of her with her fork. She clumsily dug in, getting about half of her forkful in her mouth.

This was probably the worst dinner to give Hope, as she covered the table, her clothes, and the floor in spaghetti sauce. Worse, even though she made the mess, she hated the sauce being on her hands. I had to wipe them every few seconds because she kept grabbing at her food. When I tried to take it, she screamed in protest.

Charlie and Jordan were deep in conversation. I could tell Jordan was doing his best to put on a good front with Charlie, and I liked that they were getting along, but I felt left out because of Hope's fussiness. Plus, she didn't seem like she was going to settle down anytime soon.

"I'm going to give her a bath and see if she's ready to go to bed," I said. "Do you want to say goodnight?" I asked Jordan. He looked at her, and then down at his clean clothes.

"Come get me when she's cleaned up," he said.

Hope lost her crankiness as she played with her toys in the bathtub. We were in there for a half-hour; she didn't want to leave the warm water and bubbles. I took the plug out when she wasn't looking. When the drain gurgled with the last of the water, she looked at me in confusion.

"All gone!" I said, feigning surprise. She lifted her arms up, and I wrapped her in a towel. She snuggled against me as I took her to the bedroom and dried her off before slipping her pajamas on. Then we went to say goodnight to Charlie and Jordan.

They had finished dinner, and were now in the living room. Charlie gave her a big kiss, and she squealed with delight. When he handed her to Jordan, she squirmed and reached for me.

"Guess she's still getting used to you," I said. "She's always a bit finicky before bed."

"It's okay, there's plenty of time for her to get used to me." I saw a stern look cross Charlie's face at this, but it was gone in an instant. *What's that about?*

"I'll be back," I said.

Hope went down easily, curling up on her side under her blanket.

"Goodnight baby, I love you."

"Night Mama," she murmured. I made sure the door stayed open a crack so I could hear her if she cried. Then I went to the kitchen table to eat the rest of my pasta. All of the dirty dishes were still on the table. Usually when Charlie cooked, it was my turn to clean, and vice versa. I felt overwhelmed as I surveyed the mess that was in the dining room and the kitchen. It seemed as if Charlie had used every single pot and pan, and neither he nor Jordan cleared anything from the table. I weighed the options of just leaving it for later or doing it now. I peeked around the corner at Charlie and Jordan, happy to see them getting along, but upset to be left out. Glancing back over my shoulder, I knew the logical thing was to let the kitchen wait. *They're doing fine without me*, I thought. *I'll just get this over with, and then I can visit.*

I knew I'd made the wrong decision about halfway through. Twenty minutes in, I'd managed to get the food put away and the surfaces clean. But there was still a mountain of dishes. *Leave them.* I ignored the thought and tackled the mess, carefully drying each plate and stacking them so they wouldn't chip. By the time I was done, I was beat. I retreated to the living room and sunk into the chair.

"Sorry about the mess," Charlie said. "Thank you for cleaning it up."

I was just about to answer when I heard Hope cry from her bedroom. I didn't get up right away, closing my eyes instead. I'd already wasted so much time on the kitchen. Would I be able to visit at all tonight?

"She probably just hears us talking and doesn't want to miss out." Neither of them said anything as I left.

Hope was trying to climb out of her crib. "No, you don't, little girl," I said, moving to grab her before she could throw her other leg over the railing. She cried as I tried to put her back, and stood when I took my hands away. "You're not giving in, are you?" I sighed and picked her up. She whimpered against me as I took her to the kitchen to get her sippy cup. I filled it with water and went back to the living room. Charlie and Jordan stopped talking and turned toward me as I sat down.

"She'll be tired soon if I let her stay up for a bit," I explained. Hope stayed quiet, sucking on the water. content to lean against me in my lap.

"That's fine," Charlie said. "She's not bothering anyone." He offered me a sympathetic smile. "You look exhausted."

"I'm fine. I feel bad I haven't even been able to visit."

"We've just been getting to know each other," Charlie said, smiling over at Jordan. "Seems you have quite a football fan here."

"I didn't even know you watched sports."

"When you live in a house full of guys, it's kind of inevitable," Jordan said.

"Sounds like there's plenty more for you to learn about each other," Charlie said.

"What do you mean? We like different things than we used to," I said, "but we know each other just fine."

"I bet there's a great deal you don't know," Charlie reasoned. "It's been, what, three years since you last saw each other? That's enough time for you both to change significantly."

"We haven't changed that much," I said. Charlie raised an eyebrow.

"That's not what I think. You're different than you were when you moved here. You're stronger, more independent. Not to mention, you're a mom of a toddler. Your priorities have changed. I'm willing to bet you think of your own needs less than you did before you had Hope."

"True," I conceded. "Okay, so maybe we've changed some. But we're still the same people at our core."

"Okay, let's play a game," Charlie said. It was my turn to raise an eyebrow. *A game?* What was Charlie up to? "I'm going to ask a question about the other person, and let's see how much you still know about each other."

I caught Jordan's eye, and he looked as confused as I was. Then he shot me a grin.

"This will be interesting," he said, and then gave a nervous laugh.

"Glad you think so," Charlie said. "You're first. What's Maddie's favorite animal?"

"Easy. She's always wanted a dog."

"Maddie? Is that true?"

"Still true," I said. "But less so now that I have Hope. I don't think I could handle a pet with a toddler." I looked down at Hope, who was now fighting sleep while balancing the sippy cup against her mouth.

"Well, maybe when she's older," Charlie said. "I've missed having a dog. Okay, your turn. What's Jordan's favorite food?"

"Do you still like barbecued ribs?" I asked him.

"Yup, with fat French fries on the side."

"You guys are good at this. Okay, here's a tougher one. What kind of career does the other person want? Jordan, you go first."

"Oh. Um. I don't know." Jordan studied me. "Maybe a writer?" he guessed. "She was always writing when we were younger."

"Maddie?" Charlie asked. I shook my head.

"I'm gearing up to take classes in viticulture so I can help out with the winery," I said. "And I've really grown to love gardening. But I also hope to expand on my art classes and do something that involves painting, even if it's just a hobby."

"Oh," Jordan said. "Wow. I had no idea."

"Okay, Maddie, your turn for Jordan."

"Uh." I thought back to our younger years. "Well, you worked at an auto shop in New Mexico, but I think that was just a job, not a passion. Now you work at…" I paused, looking over at Charlie. "Well, you work at a tattoo parlor." Charlie didn't look surprised. "I guess that's probably what you want as your career, and to own your own shop?"

"Yup," Jordan said.

"Okay. This question is for Maddie. What's Jordan's view on marriage?"

I shot Charlie a look.

"Well, I'm sure Jordan wants to get married one day."

"In how many years?" Charlie asked. I glanced at Jordan and saw his discomfort.

"Uh, well, not immediately," I said. "I guess in two or so years, maybe when Hope is a little older?" Jordan didn't seem any more comfortable with this timeline.

"Jordan?" Charlie prompted.

"Oh, uh, yeah. That's right."

"Fine. Jordan, how many kids does Maddie want?"

"Charlie," I warned him.

"Maddie, this is for fun. Any guesses, Jordan?"

"Uh, probably just Hope," he said. He looked at me for confirmation. I was starting to get Charlie's game, and I didn't like it. I wanted to say he was right to stack the deck. But I didn't.

"I want at least one more, maybe two," I said. Jordan shifted in his seat.

"Okay, live together before marriage?" Charlie asked Jordan.

"Um, do you want the PC answer, or the real one?" I groaned, but Charlie chuckled.

"I'm not completely naïve," he said. "I gather that means you want to move in before marriage. Is that the same for you, Maddie?"

I nodded.

"Who will do all the housework when you two live together?" Charlie asked.

"We'll split it down the middle," Jordan said

"And who will get up with Hope if she cries in the middle of the night?"

"We'll take turns."

"And what if she's sick and can't go to school? Who will stay home with her?"

"I will, unless Maddie can," Jordan answered.

"Who will make Hope's doctor's appointments? Or save for her college? Or comfort her when her heart breaks for the first time?"

"We'll both do it, okay?" Jordan spat out.

"I don't believe you," Charlie said, sitting back in his chair and folding his hands in his lap.

"What are you getting at?" I asked. "Why are you doing this?"

"It's fine, Maddie. I've had enough," Jordan said. He stood up.

"Sit down, young man," Charlie said, and I saw the rage on Jordan's face. I knew his temper. He didn't take well to demands from others. Charlie held firm, and Jordan shook his head and sat back down. "Tonight, you came over here for a meal with our family. I watched as Maddie made sure Hope was fed, bathed, and put to bed. Then she cleaned the kitchen, and tended to Hope once more. You didn't offer to help her, not once. You made me your priority when you should have made Maddie and Hope your priority. So when you say you're going to split all the responsibilities of raising a family down the middle, I don't believe you. After all, you took off three years ago and let her be responsible for raising your child on her own. What's going to stop you from leaving now?"

"I'm not leaving her!" Jordan insisted.

"Maybe not now. But what about when things get rough? What happens if money is tight? What if raising Hope isn't easy? What if you and Maddie get into a fight? Are you going to be able to stick around when things aren't new and exciting?"

"I don't have to take this," Jordan said. He got up to leave. This time, Charlie didn't stop him.

"How could you?" I demanded after Jordan slammed the door.

"Maddie, I want what's best for you. I think you deserve love and respect, to be with someone who cherishes you as an equal partner. I don't think Jordan knows how to do this."

"You don't even know him!" I yelled.

"I don't have to know him," Charlie said. "He showed me who he is in just the short amount of time he's been here. You're wrong if you think you'll have a happy family with him."

I glared at him, balancing Hope as I stood to go after Jordan.

"Let him go, Maddie."

"No, Charlie!"

He sighed. "Then give me Hope. I'll put her to bed."

"No," I said. I didn't want anything from him. As Hope stirred, though, I knew I needed to give in. I let him take Hope, and then I ran from the house to catch Jordan. He was in his car when I reached him, the engine running. I knocked on the window and he scowled, but he rolled it down.

"Come with me," he said. I shook my head.

"I can't, and you know it. Hope is in there. I'm not leaving her."

"I'm not telling you to leave her here. I'm telling you to take her and let's get out of here. You don't need Charlie. We don't need anyone but each other. We can make a life together, a family."

"Jordan."

He looked away. I jumped as he pounded the steering wheel.

"He's brainwashing you against me," he hissed. "All he sees in me is some guy with tattoos. He has no idea what I've been through, how hard I've worked, nothing. He doesn't know anything about me, and yet he's already judged who I am."

"He's just being protective of me."

"You're defending him?" Jordan looked at me, and I regretted my words.

"No! I mean, he was a jerk to you in there."

"But you believe everything he said."

"No!"

"Admit it. You think I'm some loser, and you're only with me because I'm Hope's dad."

"That's not true, and you know it."

"Then prove it. Give all this up and come with me."

"I can't."

I felt my phone vibrate in my back pocket, and I took it out. I didn't know what I was thinking. I thought it was Charlie, but my skin grew hot when I saw the text from Jace.

Jace: *Reason #5. I love spending time with you, even just as friends. I hope we can hang out again soon.*

"Who's texting you?" Jordan demanded. He grabbed the phone from me before I could respond. My body went numb as he scrolled through Every. Single. Thing. we'd texted in the past few weeks.

"It's not what you think," I said.

"Is he why you won't leave?" Jordan demanded. I shook my head. "Who is he?"

"He's a friend!" I insisted.

"I don't believe you. 'I love spending time with you, even just as friends.' It sounds like he wants a lot more than friendship with you. What have you done to make him want that?"

"Nothing!"

"I don't believe you!" Jordan slammed my phone against the dashboard. I winced as I heard it crack. He picked it up again, and smashed it repeatedly.

"Stop!" I screamed. I tried to get my phone, and he grabbed my wrist and yanked my arm through the window.

"You've been playing me this whole time," he shouted. I struggled, trying to get my hand back.

"I haven't," I insisted. He gripped me tighter, his thumb pressing into my wrist.

"I don't believe you. You had me thinking you only wanted me, but all this time you've been messing around with some other guy."

"Jordan, you're hurting me!" He looked down at my hand, then shoved it away. He picked up my phone and threw it at me. I flinched as it hit me on the shoulder and landed on the ground. The screen was shattered.

"Take your dumb phone, you bitch. I'm through with you. Go tell Charlie he was right about me and go on living in your palace." He revved his engine, narrowly missing me as he raced down the driveway.

"Jordan!" I screamed, but it was no use. He was gone. Sobbing, I picked up my smashed phone and touched the buttons. It didn't even turn on. Furious, I threw it as hard as I could down the driveway and heard it land against the gravel. Then I ran to the house.

"Maddie," Charlie said.

"Leave me alone!"

"I'm sorry. I didn't want—"

"No!" I screamed. I knew Hope was in her bedroom, probably sleeping. I didn't care. I didn't even care if I had to be up with her half the night. Nothing mattered anymore. "I will never forgive you for this."

"I only want you to be happy," he said quietly.

"No, you don't," I told him. "You wanted a servant first. And then I became your charity."

"That's not true and you know it. You're like a daughter to me."

"You're not my father!" I screamed at him. "Stop acting like you are! My real father is in New Mexico, wishing I'd never been born. You're just some guy who felt sorry for me and took me in. And now you're ruining my life! I wish I'd never met you! I wish you'd just let me die in that parking lot instead of bringing me here!"

I regretted the words immediately, especially when I saw the hurt in his eyes. My pride won out, though. I ran from the room before he could say anything else, slamming the door behind me.

I breathed hard as I leaned against the door. I longed for my phone, and then felt guilty. Even in all this, my first instinct was to call Jace.

"Jordan's right," I whispered. It was wrong of me to keep in contact with Jace. I never should have let this continue. Would I have understood if Jordan kept a friendship with a girl he was dating? No. "I've made a mess of everything."

I didn't bother getting undressed. My clothes felt damp from washing the dishes, and the spaghetti sauce splatters had probably set into the fabric. I didn't care. My head hurt from crying, and my body ached. I tried to fall asleep, but ended up in tears again as I realized I might never see Jordan again. "This is all my fault." My wrist hurt where Jordan grabbed it, but I refused to rub it. I deserved it. I practically cheated on him.

I was a failure.

Come With Me

"Maddie."

I opened my eyes and jerked back as a hand touched my shoulder.

"It's me."

"Jordan?" I felt him sit down on my bed, right in the curve of my belly. His arm stayed on my shoulder, and he embraced me.

"I'm so sorry," he murmured. "I just love you so much, it hurts sometimes." I still felt raw from our fight, but his mention of love brought me relief. In all the time I'd known him, he'd never said that—not directly, at least.

"I love you, too. And I'm sorry." In the moonlight, I saw him shake his head no.

"You didn't do anything," he said.

"Jace and I really are just friends."

"I know. I know you wouldn't cheat on me. You're not that kind of girl." He curled up against me, and I snuggled against his chest. He touched his lips to my forehead, and when I tilted my face up, he kissed my lips. He stayed there for a moment, pressing his lips to mine, then he trailed his mouth to my cheek, my neck, my collarbone. My skin felt hot, our clothes in the way. My breath was shallow as his hands pulled me closer. He brushed his lips against my ear.

"Make love to me, Maddie," he whispered. I didn't argue as he lifted my shirt above my head, and then did the same to his own. We removed the rest of our clothes and held each other skin to skin. I ran my hands over his muscled back, memorizing its peaks and valleys. His mouth found mine again, and he took me completely. We moved quietly, slowly, deeply. He paused often just to stroke my body, kiss my skin, tell me he loved me.

I lost myself to him. I lost myself in his hair, in his touch, in every word he says. For the moment, I forget about our argument. I forget that he grabbed me in a scary way and smashed my phone. I let go of the past, the one I kept trying to get over, but couldn't. In this moment, it was just him, and it was just me. *Jordan and Maddie.* We belonged together. He knew my body, my thoughts, my dreams. He knew my past. He *was* my past. Now he was my future.

He brought me to completion, waves running through me as I covered my mouth to keep silent. We finished at the same time, shuddering until we were both panting, clinging as we recovered. He moved to lie beside me, and I draped my leg over his, listening to his heartbeat.

"How did you get in here, anyway?"

"The window," he said. I looked over his body and saw how the screen was no longer there. He stroked my hair, and I felt myself starting to drift to sleep.

"Maddie, come with me."

I forced my eyes open. "Come with you *where?*"

"To Oregon. My buddy has a job and an apartment waiting for me. We can live together, and won't have to worry about anything."

"Jordan, I…" I couldn't continue. I was afraid to go with him. My home was here. I was supposed to start school in the fall. I had everything I needed to give Hope a wonderful life. But how did I tell him that? I was afraid if I told Jordan I couldn't go, he'd blow up again. Even more, I was afraid I'd lose him for good.

"I'm begging you. I want to be with you more than anything. No one makes me feel like you do. I want to be with you every day of my life, and raise a family with you. Hell, we can get married tomorrow, if you like, and start making more babies immediately."

"I don't want more babies," I said, laughing. "At least not now. And I don't want to get married yet, either."

"Then tell me what you *do* want, and I'll do it. All I'm asking is that you come with me so we can be a family. As long as you live here, it's impossible for us to be together. You know that."

I thought about what he said. It was too soon, too much, too fast, and there was so much at stake.

"What about school?"

"There's a community college in Oregon. You can go there."

"How can we afford to get there?"

"I have money. I can take care of you and Hope. I can take care of everything. Just say yes."

I closed my eyes and buried myself further into his arms, inhaling his tobacco scent.

I thought of everything that had brought me to this very moment. Three years earlier, I thought my life was over. Now, I had a life of privilege, and I didn't feel I deserved it. I earned none of this. Jordan's plan offered me a chance to make my own way with him. We could create our own life as a family. I wouldn't have to rely on anyone.

We'd be free.

But I loved this life and everyone in it. I thought about my last words to Charlie, and his pained look after I said them. He didn't deserve that. He didn't deserve someone as ungrateful as me. He didn't deserve to spend his final years taking care of a teenager and her toddler when he could be enjoying a quiet house without chaos.

Charlie had been nothing but good to me. But his views of Jordan were misguided. He didn't give him a chance. Jordan was right. If I stayed, Charlie would only get in the way of our relationship.

I no longer belonged there. I needed to live with Charlie while I couldn't take care of myself, and while he needed my help with Viola. But now that she had passed, I needed to move on. I needed to take care of myself. I couldn't be dependent on Charlie forever.

"Will you come with me?" Jordan asked. I touched his cheek, then traced my finger over his lips. He kissed my fingertips. "Say yes?"

. . .

. . .

. . .

"Yes."

To be continued.

Acknowledgements

This book, this series, has been a labor of love, from start to finish. In many ways, it's the most important series I've ever written. Knowing I'll probably never write a memoir, it's my way of telling truth through fiction.

I started the series with *The Road to Hope*, sharing themes of child loss, poverty, homelessness, and other hard topics through my characters. Maddie was an accidental character in that book, one I hadn't really planned on writing about. But soon, her world and my world started to mingle, and I couldn't get her out of my mind. Here we are, three years after I published that book, and I'm continuing her story…and in many ways, mine. *Hope at the Crossroads* was my way of sharing how confusing it is to be a young mother. Throw dating in the mix, and nothing makes sense.

Look for *Hope for the Broken Girl* in 2018, the final chapter to Maddie's story.

There are several people to thank for making this book possible.

First, my sincere and heartfelt thanks goes to Katie Watts, my tireless and devoted editor. She pored over every single word, taking out all my favorite extra words. Because of her, my characters have stopped laughing like maniacs, as well as grinning, smiling, leaning, and looking.

I want to thank my beta readers for being among my first readers, and for letting me know what needed fixing, and more important, what worked. Your feedback made for a better story, and I feel honored that you loved this story as much as I do.

To my husband, Shawn, my forever person who is always the very first to read my stories. I love that you care enough to share this with me, to mark up my manuscript with suggestions, and that you believe in me even when I don't believe in myself.

To our blended kids, Summer, Lucas, and Andrew. You are all amazing humans, and on the brink of your own life dreams. I can't wait to see what you do.

And to my God, my Creator, the One who told me to be brave and courageous because He is with me always.

Thank you is not enough. But it's a start.

Crissi's Books

The Road to Hope (Book 1 of the Hope series)

Jill Johnson loses her toddler son to an unexpected accident. Maddie Russo is a teen mother on the run, rejected by her parents and left on her own. Both have been handed a life neither was prepared for. But through one shared moment in time, they're about to change the other's life. *The Road to Hope* shares a story of overcoming tragedy and making things new from the pieces of broken lives.

Hope for the Broken Girl (Book 3 of the Hope series)

He promised to take care of her. He promised to be a good father to Hope. He promised she'd have everything she ever wanted. He lied. (Coming soon)

Loving the Wind: The Story of Tiger Lily & Peter Pan

Neverland is seen through the eyes of Tiger Lily, princess of the Miakoda Tribe. Her people share legends of the boy who flies like the birds, lives with the fairies, and harbors a stolen moon, but Tiger Lily doesn't believe the stories until she meets Peter Pan aboard Captain Hook's ship. Worse, the flying thief seems to have stolen her heart.

Come Here, Cupcake (Book 1 of the Dessert for Dinner series)

Morgan Truly never wanted to come home to Bodega Bay. But when her mother takes a turn for the worse, Morgan packs up her life in Seattle and heads back to her sleepy coastal hometown, taking on a job at the local dessert shop. She soon learns there are perks to being home. First, there's that rugged sailor who can't seem to get enough of her sweets. And second, no one else can either—because who can resist enchanted desserts? Morgan discovers she has magical abilities that involve her baking. Unfortunately, her magic is the very thing that could take her happiness away.

A Symphony of Cicadas (Book 1 of the Forever After series)

Cast into the afterlife, Rachel Ashby helplessly witnesses the remnants of the life she left behind and the undoing of her fiancé after her death. The longer she remains close, the more he falls apart. Rachel must make a choice—stay near the man she loves, or let go and move beyond.

Forever Thirteen (Book 2 of the Forever After series)

Joey Ashby died with his mother in a car accident when he was only thirteen. Being stuck forever at such an awkward age is bad enough. But when he sees the trauma his bullied best friend is facing in the world of the living, he knows he needs to step in. However, there's only so much a spirit in the afterlife can do.

Reclaim Your Creative Soul (non-fiction)

If you're a writer, artist, or musician with a full-time job or young family, you know how hard it is to find time for the creative side of your life. Through tips on organizing your space, budgeting your money, getting in touch with your spiritual side, and more, this book promises to help you find time for your craft—even if you can't quit your day job.

See all of Crissi Langwell's books at crissilangwell.com